MANDAN MESA

Hezekiah Strong was beginning to despair of finding a place where he could settle with his drovers and cattle. Then he came across Mandan Mesa, an enormous plateau. But by the time he realised that he shared his paradise with Crow Indians, he had already settled. Then there was a full-scale attack and Hezekiah and two of his men were wounded. But having found the cattleman's paradise, Hezekiah knew that, alive or dead, he would stay.

BUCK THOMPSON

◆

MANDAN MESA

Complete and Unabridged

LINFORD
Leicester

First published in Great Britain in 1996 by
Robert Hale Limited
London

First Linford Edition
published 1997
by arrangement with
Robert Hale Limited
London

British Library CIP Data

Thompson, Buck, *1916–*
  Mandan Mesa.—Large print ed.—
  Linford western library
  1. Western stories
  2. Large type books
  I. Title
  813.5′4 [F]

ISBN 0–7089–5135–X

Published by
F. A. Thorpe (Publishing) Ltd.
Anstey, Leicestershire

Set by Words & Graphics Ltd.
Anstey, Leicestershire
Printed and bound in Great Britain by
T. J. International Ltd., Padstow, Cornwall

This book is printed on acid-free paper

1

The Nights are Cold

IT wasn't like a valley which were great sunken places surrounded by mountains. Mandan Mesa stood above most of the mountains; it was a huge plateau, miles wide and deep with the scars of many winter winds to show it was high above, not below, other areas.

The Indians, long gone, had a word for such an area. It meant 'great flat place'. To the first white-eyes who saw Mandan Mesa it was the top of the world and had weather rings to prove its ancient origin. It had been there since God was young.

There were buffalo wallows to suggest that the white-eyes were not the first to discover it and stone rings where hide houses had stood, and its grass was

1

stirrup-high, to prove that it had never been overgrazed. Even after the cattle arrived the native grass flourished.

It was, as Hezekiah Strong said when he drove his first trail drive of one hundred cattle on to it, God's gift to anyone in the livestock trade.

Mandan Mesa had a number of sweetwater creeks. It was a little shy of firewood and building logs but those things were available in the surrounding mountains. The original residents of Mandan Mesa had houses of buffalo hide, their need for wood was limited to what was required for cooking and heating. Until the white-eyes arrived they did not have axes, they gathered dead-fall wood, dry as bone which gave off intense heat without smoke.

When Hezekiah brought the first cattle to the plateau he had three Texans and a wagon. It took nearly as long to find a way to get the wagon up there as it had taken to drive the longhorns the last forty miles.

Indian watched him arrive; dust rose

and the complaining cattle bawled incessantly. They had their camp at the west end of the plateau. Hezekiah set up a long day's ride to the east. He and his drovers found Indian sign but paid little attention to it; there always were tomahawks; they belonged to the land as well as bears, cougars and wolves. Not until Hezekiah's razorbacks had widened the extent of their grazing did any of them see an Indian, and all they saw was a solitary Indian atop a low rise motionless as a statue watching the drovers and the longhorns.

Hezekiah sat his saddle, occasionally making a gentle masticating motion and told his riders where there was one Indian there were more, and rode toward the mounted Indian with his Texans watching.

Hezekiah raised his right arm palm forward, the ancient sign of peace. The Indian did not move. He permitted Hezekiah to get fairly close before turning his back and loping off the knob westerly. He neither slackened his gait nor looked back.

The drovers rode up to Hezekiah, who spat amber and said, "Well, boys, he warn't friendly."

They spent the next six weeks erecting a log house. Two riders would sortie among the cattle, the other man and Hezekiah worked on the log lodge. It was springtime, they had plenty of time to finish the house even though they had to strip the wagon to its running gear and drive five miles to cut, limb and load logs.

Occasionally they'd see a mounted Indian. The last load of the logs was loaded for the drive back when they had their first encounter.

Three broncos rode across their wagon ruts and sat like statues watching. As before, when Hezekiah went forward with his hand high the Indians rode away.

When they got back with the logs one of the drovers who'd been out with the cattle had a strange story to tell as they ate by candlelight. The tomahawks had

4

killed and butchered a big dun steer, had taken the meat away and had pegged out the hide fleshside up with the head in the middle of the hide. It had an arrow through the centre of the head.

The youngest of the drovers, Johnny Tremaine, thought it was time to find the Indian camp and palaver. Hezekiah was wiping drippings from his beard when he said, "The head with the arrer in it means they're hostiles. We got to locate their camp, but on the sly. There's four of us an' gawd knows how many of them. Johnny, if us four rode into their camp we'd more'n likely never ride back."

An older rider, Douglas Hardy, grey as a badger, slitty-eyed and as tough as a boiled owl, emptied his tin cup of coffee before speaking. "It's one hell of a big mesa. For all we know them In'ians got a camp miles off. Hezekiah, you can afford to lose that dun steer. Trouble is, if they kill one an' nothin' happens they'll kill others an' we only

5

got three bulls for the cows."

Hezekiah leaned his massive body on the rickety table they'd made, to look at the older Texan. He knew each of his drovers as well as he knew the palm of his hands. Doug Hardy spoke slowly and thoughtfully. Hezekiah said, "Go on, spit it out."

"Now'n then they sneak around an' spy on us. Next time we run one down an' capture him."

For a long moment there was silence then the youngest Texan spoke. "That'd be like kickin' a hornets' nest. Like Hezekiah said, it might be a big camp. They'd come boilin' after us."

There was another moment of silence before a tall, lean man named Gus Crandal made a dry comment. "We got loopholes in every wall, plenty of vittles, plenty ammunition."

Doug Hardy looked across the table at Gus Crandal. "We drove them cattle one hell of a distance, Gus. They're all we got to seed a herd." Hardy did not elaborate because he did not have to, and he was right. If the Indians came painted for war they could probably fight them off from inside the log house, which was built like a fort, but it wouldn't be the first time frustrated tomahawks went on a rampage against cattle.

They finished their meal, emptied the coffee pot and went outside to smoke on a bench Johnny had made from a lightning-struck tree which had been split down the middle.

Hezekiah chewed as did the other older man Doug Hardy, the others rolled brown-paper cigarettes. It was cool. In time they would learn that Colorado's high country got cold at night even if the days were hot.

They did not discuss the Indians, their discussion ranged from how far the cattle would drift as they grazed to the possibility of rain, something cattlemen prayed for — if they prayed — once springtime turned to summer. Stockmen needed rain to keep the feed growing. They reminisced about events during their long drive. Drovers were not welcome in settled country where their cattle grazed off feed established stockmen claimed. There had been some hard words but no fights.

Johnny Tremaine removed his mouth organ from a shirt pocket and played. He was good with the harmonica. The music ranged from the old Confederate favourite, 'Lorena', to the 'Battle Hymn Of The Republic'. To a man they had been Confederates, but the war was a fading memory to all but the youngest rider. The others listened, felt a little homesick maybe, and by the time Hezekiah jettisoned his last cud of the day and arose they were all ready to bed down. Except Gus; he went out to lean on the pole corral they had built. The moon was close to being full, the horses had been driven in for the night after bellying-up on strong grass. They were dozing, paid no attention to the tall, lean man leaning outside listening to them.

Gus had come up hard. He'd been

orphaned in the Nations and although he was not Indian, strong impressions during his formative years had left him at odds with much he had learned during the war.

As a youngster he and Indian boys his age had hunted, trapped, and explored together. During the war he had qualified as a sharpshooter. With a carbine he was deadly accurate. With the battered old six-shooter he wore tied down, he could rarely hit a barn from the inside.

It was chilly as he leaned on the topmost stringer watching the horses. They had started out with a sizable remuda, nine using horses. While they were camped near a place called Ball's Crossing, someone had stolen three of their animals. Being freegrazers it did no good to complain to the town marshal. He had shrugged and said they shouldn't expect anything less; they were grazing over established range.

They did not get the horses back

but at a trading barn in a hamlet some days later Hezekiah had bought three horses so when they arrived on the huge plateau they again had nine animals.

Gus Crandal liked horses; having had little else in his life to cotton to, he gave his heart to animals. A man needed something to cherish; sometimes it was even a long-faced, lop-eared mule.

The chill was increasing. Gus dug out the makings to roll a smoke, his fingers slightly stiff. He rolled the quirly with great care, was twisting the ends before popping the thing between his lips to light it when one of the horses threw up its head and softly snorted.

Gus froze. The other horses were unconcerned. Gus lipped the quirly, tucked the sack and papers back into a shirt pocket when the nervous horse stamped and took a step backwards, little ears pointing dead ahead. Several other animals either saw or scented something and also lined up to peer into the night.

Gus did not light the quirly. He tugged loose the tie-down thong over his holstered Colt and very gently faced northward, the direction the horses were staring.

There were mountain lions, bears and wolves, but this was different; horses stampeded at the first scent of a large varmint. These horses were poised to whirl but they didn't.

Gus saw nothing, heard nothing and sighted no movement but for a fact there was something. Horses were bolters by nature but these horses stood their ground and for a fact *something* had their full attention.

Gus knew how silent and wily wolves were. He'd also had his share of encounters with bears. He'd shot a mountain lion trying to hamstring horses in a corral years back.

He speculated that it was a pack of wolves but try as he did he could not make out movement. The grey horse who had originally got his ruff up sidled slightly toward the area where

11

Gus was standing. Another horse also sidled westerly. Gus strained to catch movement on the north side of the corral. For a long time, with the cold increasing, he detected nothing. On a night, cold or not, the best way to detect danger of any kind was by watching for movement. Even with a nearly full moon Gus was unable to see what had upset the horses, but something surely had. All nine animals were now rigidly staring in one direction — northerly.

Gus slowly fisted his six-gun, otherwise he did not move, did not make a sound. The hair on the back of his neck was rising. He forgot about the cold.

The last candle had been snuffed out at the house, there wasn't a sound. Gus waited. It was a long wait but eventually he heard it; something moving from the east toward the corral. It was a slow and deliberate sound, the kind a mountain lion might make, but not a bear or wolves.

He switched the Colt to his left hand

in order to wipe palm-sweat on his britches before regripping the gun in his right hand.

Very slowly it dawned on Gus what was happening. He gradually and very slowly hunkered until he could see the east side of the corral. Mostly, his view was interrupted by the legs of horses but twice he detected movement which he might not have been able to detect if there had been no moon.

The movement was blurry and there were frequent pauses, but each time he saw movement the wraith was edging around toward the south side of the corral where the gate was.

Gus lay a hand on the bottom-most corral stringer to retain balance as he inched toward the south-west corner of the corral. What helped was the horses; they were shifting position in order to keep track of the wraith.

Each time horses moved so did Gus. When he reached the corner of the corral he could make out nothing but the faint sound of something moving.

It was little more than a whisper of sound.

He had to dry his sweaty palm again. Somewhere an owl hooted. Gus froze until it was answered by another owl some distance northward.

He got belly down, left his hat aside and peered around the logs in the direction of the gate, which was secured by an old harness chain and snap.

Finally, as the wraith edged around toward the gate on the south side Gus could make out details. It was an Indian with roached hair, a fleshing knife on his belt and a pistol holster from which the top flap had been cut off exposing the stock.

Gus gauged the distance and gathered both legs for the spring when he arose to fire. The Indian did something unexpected. He undoubtedly saw the chain. Instead of releasing the snap he passed completely past the gate to within less than fifty feet from where Gus was crouching. He leaned on the topmost stringer looking in at the horses. Gus had two seconds to think this tomahawk was a selective horsethief. He'd never run across a horsethief who was selective, it was their custom to come in fast, make a gather and leave in a dead run.

While the Indian was leaning against the topmost stringer, both arms hooked across the topmost sapling, Gus came up off the ground as though he had come out of it. The Indian caught movement instantly. His mistake was that shock, or something anyway, held him motionless as Gus came at the Indian handgun swinging. At the last moment the Indian tried to twist clear. Gus's pistol barrel missed the head but came down with considerable force on the Indian's shoulder. The pain had to be intense but the bronco did not make a sound. He was right-handed, the blow had numbed his right arm but he tried to draw his six-gun. Gus's second strike put the Indian face down with blood showing through his roached hair. If he hadn't been roached the blood might not have shown so swiftly.

Gus leaned, plucked away the old hawgleg and the wicked-bladed big fleshing knife and straightened up.

He was standing like that looking down when a drawling voice came out of the darkness behind him. Gus whirled six-gun rising.

Doug Hardy spoke sharply, "Aim that gun away. It's me." There was a pause before Hardy spoke again. "What you got there, an Indian?"

Gus leathered his sidearm and also gazed at the unconscious Indian. "He was fixin' to open the gate, run the horses out an' set us afoot."

"Is he dead?"

"I don't know."

Hardy sank to one knee, raised a hand and said, "You hit him over the head with your gun barrel?"

"Yes."

"He's bleedin' like a stuck hawg."

"Let the son of a bitch bleed. If

16

he'd run off our horses we'd have been sittin' ducks next time they come skulkin' around."

Doug Hardy stood up, pulled grass to wipe blood off his hand and wagged his head. "Did you ever hear it said where there's one varmint there's more?"

Gus turned his head for the first time since Doug had appeared. As he turned it back he said, "How come you to be out here? There wasn't hardly no noise."

"I had to pee . . . he's your In'ian, what'd you want to do with him?"

"Shoot the son of a bitch!"

Doug reacted as though that statement hadn't been seriously made. "Well; Johnny's right. We got a hostage. Lend me a hand packin' him to the lodge."

Gus lent a hand but was not at all in agreement with the idea of a hostage.

They got him inside where it was as dark as the inside of a boot and while Doug foraged for a candle and lighted it Gus held the unconscious Indian on a bench.

Doug went to Hezekiah's bunk and kicked it. The bearded face that emerged from the blankets looked puffy in the puny light. Hezekiah said, "It ain't sunup."

Hardy leaned, jerked his thumb over his shoulder as he said, "We got an In'ian."

Hezekiah's sleep-fogged eyes cleared. He sat straight up and peered. "Dead, is he?"

"No, but got a pretty bad cut on the head where Gus hit him with his hand-gun."

Hezekiah pushed out of his blankets, leaned to tug on his boots and said, "I thought we figured it warn't a good idea to catch one?"

From across the room Gus said, "He was fixin' to open the gate and set us afoot. I didn't have no choice. Maybe he'll die; he bled a lot an' ain't come around yet. I didn't hit him all that hard."

Doug rolled his head. "You hit him hard. If he didn't have a cast-iron skull you'd have killed him."

Hezekiah was buttoning his britches when he said, "Light another candle."

2

The Hostage

BY the time they had doused the Indian with cold water and patted mud over his torn scalp Johnny Tremaine was pulling on his britches and boots. One of them lighted another candle.

Their Indian was young, somewhere in his late teens. His was muscular, lean as a cougar and had some kind of tattoo on his chest and back.

They examined the fleshing knife and old hawgleg pistol. Gus held the gun close to a candle and said, "U.S." He tossed the weapon on the table and gazed at the Indian. "Maybe his pappy got it. He's too young. That gun's as old as he is."

Doug was still worried about more Indians being out in the night. He

20

thought someone should go out to the corral and mind the horses. Hezekiah thought that was a good idea and sent Gus. When he hesitated at the door Johnny Tremaine crossed over. They departed together.

Hezekiah got a cud cheeked, ran a set of bent fingers through his awry hair and sat down at the table. Their Indian was limp as a rag and unconscious. Hezekiah said, "Get a few swallows of whiskey down him."

After that was done without incident, the Indian belched, raised a sluggish arm toward his face and opened both eyes. The arm stopped moving, the eyes widened. He looked from bearded, massive Hezekiah to Doug Hardy, to his weapon atop the table and back to Hezekiah, who addressed the young bronco.

"Did you bring friends to help steal our horses?"

The Indian looked blankly at Hezekiah.

Doug sighed. "Don't know English."

Hezekiah sucked his tobacco without taking his eyes off the young Indian. He said, "What kind of bronco you figure him to be, Doug?"

Hardy had no idea. This was Colorado. Where he had grown up he could identify Indians off hand. He said, "What Indians they got here? I can tell you what he ain't. That's all I can tell you." He went to a bench and sat down. "They'll come lookin' for him, I'll bet a new hat on that."

First light brightened the big plateau from east to west. Johnny and Gus returned. They had neither seen nor heard Indians. The corralled horses evidently hadn't either, they were dozing and relaxed.

While they were making breakfast Johnny tried talking with the Indian. Either their hostage could not, or would not, speak English. Doug thought he could not.

They gave him a tin plate of antelope meat, bread as hard as dry mud and coffee. He held the plate and cup but made no attempt to eat or drink. Hezekiah examined the head wound. There was no bleeding but there was a knot up there as large as a hen's egg. He told the others the bronco more than likely had a headache to end all headaches.

With the sun climbing they left Johnny to guard the hostage, got a-horseback and went out among the cattle. They did not see a single Indian.

On the ride back Doug speculated on how far the rancheria was. His conclusion was that, given the size of the mesa, it could be as much as twenty miles westerly. It was a good guess.

When they got back and had cared for their animals a solitary Indian appeared from the north riding a grey horse with something only one of the Texans had ever seen before. Each ear had been split, both halves had then been rolled down and evidently tied until they healed. The appearance was of a horse with a pair of fuzz balls on each side of its head.

Doug Hardy watched the Indian and abruptly said, "Crow!" The others gazed from the approaching rider to their companion. Hezekiah said, "You sure?" Hardy was sure. "I seen 'em once in New Messico. It was a raidin' party. They rode into a bushwhack set up by a posse of townsmen. Killed four, caught two wounded ones an' the others scattered like birds."

Hezekiah leaned, spat, eyed the Indian and shook his head. "That'd be a nice animal except for them ears."

Doug was still squinting when he said, "That's how I knew. They had them balled-up ears when they made that raid."

The Indian was an older man but muscular. His nose was beaked like a hawk. He mouth was a bloodless slit and his hair was roached with a single, notched feather tied into the hair. He rode with a Winchester across his lap. He wore beaded cuffs on each arm between the elbow and the shoulder. He was armed with a Colt on the right side and a knife on the left side.

Gus scanned east and west, ended up looking northward. He had been told where there are lice there are nits. He loosened his six-gun and watched the Indian halt about fifty yards away.

Hezekiah raised his right hand, palm forward. The Indian returned the salute but belatedly and grudgingly. He called in a deep voice. "You see In'ian?"

Hezekiah gave an oblique answer. "Every few days we see In'ians."

The iron-jawed Indian fixed Hezekiah with a glare as black as midnight. "One In'ian boy."

"What's his name?"

"Absaroke name Long Walker."

"Why would we see him?"

The black eyes never left Hezekiah. "He come here last night. He don't come back."

"Why did he come here?"

The black eyes narrowed. "You talk much, say nothing . . . where is boy?"

Hezekiah leaned to expectorate. The Indian watched and said, "You have bad blood. Spit dirt."

Doug Hardy stifled an urge to laugh. Hezekiah gazed at the bronco, fished out his plug and rode closer with the plug held on his palm. The Indian squinted, leaned to sniff and straightened back. "White man poison."

Hezekiah pocketed the plug, gazed thoughtfully at the Indian and said, "Long Walker come in the night to steal our horses."

"Where is he?"

Doug glanced sharply at Hezekiah. The bronco would not have asked where the youth was if he had thought the Texans had killed him. In other words there had indeed been other Indians with Long Walker. When they had returned without him they could say there had been no gunshot.

Hezekiah jerked his head in the direction of the log house. "He got hit on the head."

The Indian looked in the direction of the house for a long moment before speaking.

"You let him go."

Hezekiah inclined his head. "Be right glad to, when you give your word won't no more In'ians try to steal our horses."

The other older man glared. "You no belong here. This our land."

Hezekiah did not reply, he reined back where his Texans sat, faced around, gave glare for glare with the Indian, then said, "Let's go," and led off in the direction of the log house. Gus Crandal rode twisted looking back, the Indian sat his horse stone-faced watching. As the Texans dismounted to care for their horses the Indian rode back the way he had come.

Inside, Johnny Tremaine had made a meal. As the men filed in to eat Johnny said, "He knows English. His name is Long Walker. He meant to run off the horses to prove his manhood."

No one spoke until they had eaten then Gus told Hezekiah what he had deduced, there had been other broncos with Long Walker.

Hezekiah arose, went to lean and examine the Indian's wound, straightened up and said, "An In'ian come lookin' for you. Old as I am, had a notched feather."

Long Walker looked up. "Ride grey horse?"

Hezekiah nodded. "Who is he?"

"Black Thunder."

Hezekiah continued to regard the hostage as he dryly said, "The name fits. I offered to let you go if he'd pass his word they wouldn't try to run off our horses. He wouldn't give his word. Tell me somethin', are you a Crow?"

Long Walker nodded gingerly. His headache had diminished but other pains lingered. "Absaroke."

"That's the same as Crow?"

Long Walker gave another slight nod.

Hezekiah dug out his plug, gnawed

off a corner and cheeked it with Long
Walker watching. As Hezekiah put the
plug in a pocket he said, "Where is
your camp?"

Long Walker was mute and impassive.
Hezekiah returned to the table and
refilled his tin cup. Gus Crandal jerked
his head. They went outside where the
lanky man said, "Put him out front.
Go back-trackin' the old bronco until
we find their camp."

"What for?"

"Trade the bronco for his pa's word
they won't kill no more cattle."

Hezekiah turned aside, expectorated
and turned back. "In'ian's word ain't
worth a damn."

"We got the lad. They ain't goin'
to cause trouble if they figure we'll
shoot him. All right. Let things slide
for a few days then take him over
an' make a trade." Crandal's eyes
narrowed. "Hezekiah, we can't stand
losin' no more cattle, specially bulls'n
cows, an' them In'ians live up here too.
We got to get some kind of agreement

with 'em. If we don't we might as well tuck tail an' hunt another place to settle in."

Hezekiah jettisoned his cud, spat and leaned to gaze at the cloudless sky. "We should've scouted up the mesa first."

Gus nodded. "But we didn't an' this is as good a cow country as we're likely to ever find. Hezekiah, I'm gettin' too long in the tooth to go on wanderin', an' gettin' run off for bein' a freeway grazer, an' so are you. We got the young buck, his pa wants him back. You're a horse-trader. You know what I'm sayin'."

Hezekiah reared back to reconsider the cloudless sky. "In the damned mornin'," he said. "Tell the lad we're takin' him home. He'll lead us to the damned camp . . . I'm tired." Hezekiah turned back to enter the house.

Gus's idea had been to let the tomahawks sweat for a few days but he settled for Hezekiah's idea to hunt up the rancheria the following day.

Hezekiah asked Long Walker how far the Indian camp was before retiring. What the young bronco had told him made him tell the others they would leave before dawn in the morning.

They put Long Walker on a bareback horse. He said nothing. When Hezekiah told him to lead the way to the rancheria, he still said nothing but he nodded.

It was a long ride. They covered about half the distance before sunrise. Johnny Tremaine rode stirrup with the Indian. They conversed occasionally. Hezekiah told Gus, Johnny and Long Walker had more in common than the older riders had and Gus nodded.

Visibility was excellent, the land was flat, new-day warmth made for comfortable riding. Only once did they stop, that was at a creek to water the animals. Here, when Long Walker started to dismount Doug Hardy growled for him to stay astride. Johnny told the older man Long Walker had to pee. Doug was unrelenting.

When they left the creek Johnny's indignation lingered. He told Hardy their prisoner couldn't have run off. There wasn't even a tree in sight. Doug did not respond.

With heat increasing Hezekiah wrinkled his nose. "Smoke," he told Gus. "We're gettin' close."

But they did not see the camp for another couple of miles. What they saw kept the Texans silent. There were at least two dozen hide tipis. A number of noisy youngsters were out with the loose stock. They didn't see the riders but an old woman who had been slapping wet clothes on rocks beside a creek saw them and made a high, trilling sound.

The camp erupted. Women and children ducked into tipis, men, both old and young appeared with weapons. They faced Hezekiah's riders without speaking or moving. Gus made a rough count and leaned to speak to Hezekiah. "Fifty, sixty of 'em."

Hezekiah did not respond, he was seeking Black Thunder among the warriors.

Long Walker spoke to Johnny Tremaine and raised an arm. Johnny called back to Hezekiah. "In front of that hide tent with the buffler head painted on it."

Hezekiah altered his course a fraction, heading for the spokesman he had met the day before. Doug Hardy surreptitiously loosened the tie-down over his holstered Colt. Long Walker jerked his head for Johnny Tremaine to follow and broke over into a lope in the direction of the buffalo-head tipi. Black Thunder saw him. When they were close enough Long Walker called ahead. The older man neither responded nor showed expression. If he was glad to see the youth there was no indication. His jaw was set, his eyes barely acknowledged Long Walker, they were fixed on Hezekiah.

The Texans drew rein near the line of Indians, sat their saddles considering the camp of war-ready Indians. The man they thought was Long Walker's father said, "Get down."

The Texans dismounted. They stood close to their animals. If there was a fight they could swing the horses sideways for protection.

Long Walker swung to the ground near Black Thunder and spoke rapidly in guttural bursts. The old man did not take his eyes off Hezekiah, who was the centre of attention, not only because of his size and heft but also because of his full beard.

Black Thunder finally exchanged words briefly with Long Walker then banished him to the tipi behind them. Gus spoke aside to Hezekiah. "I think he's mad because the lad didn't set us afoot an' got caught."

Hezekiah handed Gus his reins, and tugged off his gloves as he approached the Indian. From a distance of about sixty feet he said, "He's got a cut on the head, otherwise he ain't been harmed."

The Indian did not speak.

Hezekiah folded the gloves over and under his shell belt. "We trade," he told the stone-faced Indian. "We give you back the boy, you leave us be."

A tall, lithe young Indian carrying a Winchester rifle in the crook of one arm said, "You don't belong here. This land belongs to us."

Hezekiah considered this tomahawk. He had only a barely discernible guttural accent to his English. Hezekiah said, "You got a name?"

"Squawman. You got a name?"

"Hezekiah Strong." Hezekiah tipped his head toward Long Walker's father. "What's his name?"

"Absaroke, that's the name of our people. His name's Black Thunder."

Hezekiah dug out his plug, bit off a corner, cheeked it and expectorated. The Indians watched impassively until Squawman spoke again.

"You got to leave."

Hezekiah considered the lean Indian without speaking until Black Thunder did so, harshly. "You go! You go by full moon."

Hezekiah swung his attention to the speaker, spat aside and answered shortly. "It's a big mesa, plenty of room for us an' you, an' Mister, you kill one more of our critters an' we'll bring in the army."

Squawman spoke before Black Thunder could. "This is our place. Our enemies are many, Hidatsa, Cheyenne, Assinboin from up north. Here, we can see enemies coming for many miles. This is our home. You go."

A small Indian boy, no more than five or six years old, escaped from his mother and ran toward Hezekiah. He stopped dead still looking up. Hezekiah smiled slightly and stroked his beard. The child laughed.

Gus sank to one knee. The child went to him. Gus fished in a pocket for a scrap of licorice root, gave it to the child and put his own finger in his mouth. The child did the same. His face brightened. He sucked the licorice root and smiled at Gus until his mother pushed past, picked him up and went back among the tipis.

Squawman and Black Thunder exchanged a look. The older man was about to speak when the tall younger Indian spoke first. "You round up cattle and go away. If you don't we will shoot your cattle and take your horses."

Long Walker came through the motionless warriors with one hand outstretched. He did not smile or speak as he handed Johnny Tremaine some cured wild apples.

Black Thunder snarled and Long Walker obediently went back among the tipis. The old man spoke to Squawman who interpreted. "You are enemies. We don't need no more enemies. Spokesman say for you to go now. Go get your cows and go away with them."

Hezekiah faced Black Thunder. "Among us, when a man does a favour to someone, like not killin' your son an' fetchin' him back to you, we figure it's a matter of honour for someone like you to show you owe us."

Squawman repeated what Hezekiah had said in Crow, although the old spokesman probably understood. He gazed a long moment at Hezekiah before speaking.

"You take two moons, not one, to go away with your animals. Two moons."

He abruptly turned and walked back to the tipi with the buffalo head painted on it. He ducked to enter and did not reappear.

Squawman said, "Two moons. That's two months. Absaroke repays you. Now go."

Hezekiah considered the line of unsmiling, armed warriors, shrugged, mounted his horse and said, "You kill another of my critters an' I'll hunt up the army an' lead 'em back here." He turned and led the way back.

There was very little conversation until they reached that warm-water creek where they had watered the livestock before, there, they dismounted, drank, splashed water over their faces and allowed the horses to drag their reins and crop feed while the men sat beside the creek to smoke and chew jerky. Doug asked Gus where he'd got that licorice root.

Crandal was chewing a long stalk of sweet-grass when he replied. "Dug it out a week or so back an' set it to cure. I got more if you want some."

Doug declined, he had pouched a chew into his cheek shortly before they reached the creek. He thumbed back his hat as he gazed at Gus. "You sure made a friend with that In'ian kid."

Johnny ate dried wild apples, but only because he was hungry. Wild apples, not much larger than a child's fist, cured or tree-ripened, were as pithy and bitter as original sin.

Johnny waited until the others were ready to ride before he threw the remainder of Long Walker's gift into the creek.

3

Indians!

HEZEKIAH was out front on the bench watching Johnny Tremaine with their grazing horses when Gus came from around back, sat down and said, "Two months."

Hezekiah grimaced. "They'll kill more cattle. It's easier'n huntin' meat."

Gus did not dispute this. He wasn't thinking of the cattle. He was thinking of what he'd said to Hezekiah much earlier. "This here's as good a place to settle as we're goin' to find. Like I told you, this wanderin' through mountains lookin' for a settlin' down place can go on until snow flies without findin' anythin' better."

Hezekiah looked around. He and Gus had been together three years. He relied on Gus in many ways. "You heard the old bronco. Two moons. Don't talk to me about comin' to a meetin' of minds with that In'ian."

Gus sighed, arose and entered the log house. Hezekiah returned to watching the youngest Texan drive the horses in to be corralled for the night. Behind him someone had a supper fire going. He could smell the smoke rising above their log house.

Johnny came over, sat down to remove his spurs and put a sidelong glance on Hezekiah's bearded and solemn countenance before speaking. "It's mighty fine stock country," he said, leaning back. "Give us a few years an' we could increase the herd to five times what we got. Good feed, plenty of water."

"An' In'ians," Hezekiah said.

"Do like you said, go back yonder, find an army post 'n lead soldiers back up here. They got reservations where they corral In'ians."

Hezekiah sat loose on the bench. Inside two men were talking. Whatever

41

they were discussing was indistinguishable to the men outside on the bench.

Johnny went to work rolling a smoke. After lighting it he spoke again. "Sure hate to leave this place. Look out yonder. There's everythin' folks need to set up with seed stock. Best place I've seen since I hired on. Maybe you could talk terms with them tomahawks. Folks been talkin' 'em out of land for a long time. Or let the army handle it. Hell, they'd make jerky out of them warriors. Then we could set to work settlin' in an' prosperin'."

Hezekiah had been considering the scuffed toes of his boots throughout this one-sided discussion. Now, he moved both feet slightly and spat between them. "Johnny, you remember how folks ganged up an' run us off for bein' free-grazers?"

"I do for a fact. There was times I figured someone'd get shot."

"I ain't goin' for the army."

The younger man's eyes widened.

"There's a heap of In'ians an' not many of us."

This conversation ended when Doug Hardy appeared in the doorway to announce supper was ready.

Johnny repeated what Hezekiah said to the others when they were making one of their almost daily sweeps out where the cattle were. Doug shook his head. Gus did not do that but he looked at the broad back of Hezekiah riding up ahead, and sighed.

They lost no more cattle, which Hezekiah attributed to the possibility of good hunting over the countryside, and he was probably right. Spring, summer and autumn were good hunting months.

Nor did they see any tribesmen for about two weeks after Black Thunder's ultimatum until the day Long Walker appeared, riding a red roan horse with an eagle feather braided into its mane up near the right ear. The roan horse's ears had not been cropped.

Hezekiah recognised the youth from

a distance and sang out that Johnny had a visitor. Tremaine called out and raised his gun-hand — the right one — palm forward. Long Walker did the same and kneed his red roan into a trot.

The men on the porch watched, stiff as statues, as Johnny and the Crow met. Long Walker slid to the ground and squatted. Once, the older man heard laughter and Gus said, "Too bad it ain't Black Thunder."

Long Walker gave Johnny something, got back astride and rode westerly. Johnny returned to the porch holding up a brace of mountain quail, not enough for all the Texans but at least a good gesture.

After supper Johnny went outside to make a smoke. Doug told Gus whatever Johnny and the bronco had talked about had made an impression on the youngest among them.

Gus went out and sat on the bench. If he was waiting for Johnny to speak it was a long wait so Gus finally spoke.

"You got a friend."

Johnny nodded. "He said they won't bother the livestock no more. He said their spokesman is making notches on a stick for when two moons has passed."

"And . . . ?"

"He said his people ain't liked by other In'ians. He told me the big bellies is on the move southward from Montana. He said his pa sent scouts to see if they come down here or if they veer off. If they come here, find the Crows, there'll be a fight."

Johnny looked at Gus. "I asked him why other In'ians don't like Crows. He told me a long time ago the Crows stole women from the other In'ians. He said that's when it started. He said there are other tribes that hate his people. It sounded to me like they don't have no friends."

"Who these oncomin' In'ians?"

"He said big bellies. You ever heard of In'ians called big bellies?"

Gus hadn't. "No, but up here they got different In'ians than down in

45

Texas and New Messico. We heard you laughing . . . ,"

"He said when he come to steal our horses it was his first time, an' what he was told was that white-eyed people was easy to raid, an' touched his head. That's when we laughed. Gus . . . ?"

"Yep."

"You was in the war."

Crandal didn't answer, he nodded slightly and gazed in the direction of the corral.

"I once heard an old Yankee say there aren't no winners, just them that live through."

Gus leaned back. "That's about right."

"We're to hell an' gone from towns, nothin' but them Crows 'n us, some cougars, bears an' what not. It's one hell of a big mesa."

Gus interrupted. "Johnny, I know it don't make sense but as long as us animals eat meat we'll fight. Did he say how many of them other In'ians

46

is comin' down this way?"

"No."

Gus slapped the youth on the leg, shot up to his feet and said, "By my calculations we still got about a month." He was turning to go back inside when he hesitated and also said, "Where there's only one man left he'll fight his shadow," and went inside where Hezekiah was squinting through some steel-rimmed spectacles and looked up. Gus repeated only what Johnny had said about the Crows, and some other tomahawks coming southward from up north.

Hezekiah removed the glasses and rubbed his eyes. There were four candles burning. Doug was sitting close to one candle slicing gnarled lengths of licorice root into pocket-sized pieces. Without looking up he said, "Might not be a bad idea to keep a close watch on the livestock."

Hezekiah arose, carefully folded the eyeglasses into their steel case and headed for his bunk as he replied to Doug Hardy. "More gawddamned In'ians."

Gus and Hezekiah packed one horse and left Doug and Johnny to mind things while they went searching for another place to settle.

They had been gone two days before Black Thunder and that tall Crow named Squawman rode to the clearing of the log house.

Squawman did most of the talking, Doug and Johnny did most of the listening. Black Thunder stood impassively hostile, for the most part with nothing to say.

Squawman did not use the bench, nor did Black Thunder. Doug and Johnny did. Squawman spoke English with scarcely a trace of an accent. He said, "The other two rode away with a pack horse. Where?"

Doug answered candidly. "To find a place for us to go when we got to leave here."

Black Thunder glared at Doug and said, "No!"

Squawman said something to Black Thunder in their own language and although the spokesman continued to glare he said no more, but Squawman did. "They rode north," he said and gestured in that direction with an upraised arm.

Doug nodded.

Again Black Thunder stiffened, but in anticipation Squawman brushed the spokesman with his hand, then addressed the seated men again. "Long Walker told you the Gros Ventres are coming south."

Both Texans gazed blankly at the tall Indian. Johnny said, "He told me some In'ians called big bellies was coming south."

Squawman considered Johnny. "Gros Ventres are Lakota. They are called big bellies. Your friends went to find them, lead them to our camp."

It dawned on Doug, but not on Johnny, the reason for this visit and the fierce bearing of Black Thunder. He shook his head. "They went lookin' for a place to take the cattle after we got to leave here, an' that's the gospel truth. They don't know anythin' about the big bellies or whatever you call 'em."

"They rode north," Squawman said again, and Doug's temper flared. "For Chris' sake that don't mean they won't go east or west, does it? Mister, I'll tell you for a damned fact we're up to our butts with our own trouble. We ain't interested in In'ians, your kind or any other kind." Doug glared at Black Thunder. "Hezekiah an' Gus went lookin' for another place for us to settle in with the cattle. They ain't lookin' for In'ians. We seen enough of In'ians since Long Walker tried to set us afoot."

Doug arose and Johnny, who had known Hardy several years sat like a stone looking up. He had never seen Doug this angry before.

Squawman spoke aside to Black Thunder. The spokesman relaxed enough to lean on a porch upright when he spoke. "If you lie we come back. Kill all of you, set fire to your home and take all your animals."

Squawman waited until the spokesman was leaving the porch to address Doug again. "I grew up among whites. They are big liars. Not all but many."

"I'm not lyin'!" Doug exclaimed, mad enough to fight.

Squawman followed Black Thunder to their horses, got astride and did not look back.

Doug sat down and slumped, as he and Johnny watched the Indians ride westward. Johnny said, "Gawddamned In'ians got more names for each other than a man can shake a stick at."

Doug responded by going inside and taking two long pulls on the whiskey jug.

Three days later Hezekiah and Gus returned. Atop the diamond hitch of the pack horse was a large five-point buck Hezekiah had shot with his handgun when they aroused it out of its bed. They had gutted it but had not skinned it.

While the skinning was in progress Doug related the visit of Black Thunder and the tall bronco. Gus said nothing. He was peeling back the skin as he cut it loose so that no hair touched the meat, otherwise the meat would taste strong. It was Hezekiah who startled both Doug and Johnny. "How far off was they?" he asked Crandal who answered without missing a cut with his fleshing knife. "Two days ride."

Doug said, "In'ians?"

"Yep. Johnny, put a rag over your shoulder and pack this quarter inside."

Johnny did not move. "Two days ride? Comin' in this direction?"

Hezekiah wiped his knife and scowled. "Get this meat inside before the damned flies blow it. Yep, two days ride."

Doug asked how many and Gus paused at wiping his bloody hands and forearms to reply. "We stayed far off, but it was a big straggle of 'em."

Johnny was hopeful as he took the quarter of meat on his shoulder.

"Maybe they'll veer off."

Gus agreed. "Maybe. If they don't an' they come visitin' Black Thunder's folks, it's goin' to be one hell of a big — "

Doug blurted out that the oncoming tribesmen were bitter enemies of the Crows, and now Gus raised his eyes. Hezekiah looked steadily at Doug. "How do you know that?"

"I already told you," Doug replied. "Black Thunder an' that skinny one figured you'n Gus went to find them big bellies an' fetch 'em back here to attack the Crows."

"I didn't understand you to say no such a thing."

Gus spoke before tempers flared. "Hezekiah, we ain't in a real good place if there's a big Indian fight. Fightin' In'ians is crazy, even if they don't come this far to attack us too, sure as Hell's hot they'll wipe out the cattle."

Johnny came back for the next quarter which Hezekiah placed over his shoulder, then spat out his cud and swore.

They finished with the deer, pegged its hide to the front of their log house flesh side out so the flies would glean the remaining shreds of meat, cleaned up at the creek which ran through one corner of the corral and went inside.

Doug fired up the cook stove, which was in one corner, made of rocks held in place by mud mixed with 'corral dust' while Hezekiah took the jug to the table with him, sat down and repeated something he'd said earlier.

"Gawddamned In'ians!"

They ate with dusk settling. Not much was said until later, when the candles had been lighted, then Doug, still rankled at Hezekiah, said, "Did you find another place for the cattle?"

Hezekiah did not look at Hardy when he replied, "There is nothin' between this place an' as far as we went but mountains, an' we climbed a couple of peaks to see further — all we seen was that big band of In'ians raisin' enough dust to blot out the sun, and more damned mountains."

Hezekiah glanced at Crandal as though seeking confirmation, but Gus was not thinking of their fruitless search, he was thinking of Indians in this isolated place, dozens of their fighting men and this log house with only four defenders — and the cattle. He pushed back off the table and looked squarely at Hezekiah.

"Back the way we come," he said, "there was some places with good feed."

Hezekiah snorted. "You know better. All the good graze is taken up. It'd be like kickin' a beehive for us to go back down there. Them folks'd be after us like the devil after a crippled saint."

Gus nodded. "An' if we stay here?"

Hezekiah pushed the jug across toward Gus as he said, "My old ma wanted me to settle in a town, open a smithy, marry a wide-hipped woman and live a respectable life."

Gus was not in the mood to be

put off with that kind of talk so he answered sharply, "So you're goin' to set up here until the warwhoops lift your hair. We come one hell of a distance with the cattle. We can run for it, stay here an' get killed, or face civilised cowmen down out of here, an' still have the cattle an' keep our hair."

Doug went out to the bench to study the summer night. Johnny joined him out there. He said, "Maybe they will veer off."

Doug snorted. "Johnny, In'ians on the move is like armies, they put out scouts an' skirmishers in all directions. If they're two days off that means that by tomorrow night their scouts will have found this mesa — and the Crows — an' us."

"Then we'd better do like Gus said, get the hell back south as fast as we can."

From the doorway Hezekiah said, "We'll round up the cattle in the mornin'." He also said, "A hunnert animals movin' in a bunch'll put up a dust them tomahawks'll see for ten miles." Hezekiah came to sit beside Johnny. "You ride to the Crow camp first thing. Tell 'em what Gus an' I seen, then get back as quick as you can because Doug, Gus'n me'll have the cattle bunched."

Doug arose to stroll out and lean on the corral. To a stockman no other sound or smell was as pleasurable. He was still out there when Gus came out. They shared a plug of molasses cured before Gus said, "Between a rock an' a hard place."

Doug replied quietly. "We'll never get the critters gathered and ready to drive in time, Gus. If we try all we'll end up doin' is get caught between two bunches of damned In'ians."

"Hezekiah wouldn't leave the cattle behind, Doug. He's been a long time puttin' 'em together. They're his last chance."

Doug turned discreetly to expectorate before speaking again. "Before you come up I was thinkin' of somethin'. Suppose a couple of us snuck back where them In'ians is comin' and fired the countryside. That'd ought to make them turn back or go in some other direction."

4

A Long Day,
a Longer Night

JOHNNY left in the dark. It was a long ride over and a long ride back. The others ate sparingly, went to the corral and rigged out without talking. The animals they didn't use they left corralled.

If there had been a moon it was not up there when the riders left the yard. Normally Gus would have uncharitable thoughts about hunting cattle in the dark, but this time their shared sense of urgency prevented Crandal from dwelling on anything but the chore ahead.

They knew about where the cattle were, which helped, but there was always drift so, although they found many animals still in their beds there were others they had to sashay in different directions before finding them, pushing them back to the gather, and by first light Hezekiah thought they may have missed a few but he was content. For one thing they had found all three bulls.

They had the cattle bunched about three miles northwest of the log-house clearing. They began the drive slowly, the only way half-wild range cattle could be herded. It they were hurried they panicked and bolted every which way.

Hezekiah's crew were experienced drovers. They should have been, they'd been looking at the rear-ends of these critters a very long time.

They had to drift the cattle toward the creek, which annoyed Hezekiah, but cattle drank early. Doug and Gus stood with their animals. Hezekiah walked toward them leading his animal. When he was close he said, "I worry a tad about the lad."

Doug offered reassurance. "He'll be

all right. We'll meet him down the trail somewhere."

Hezekiah responded dryly. "One time I read in a book that it was the custom in other countries to kill a messenger who brought bad news."

Neither Doug nor Gus responded, for one thing some of the cattle had tanked up and were looking around for graze.

By the time the drive had the log house in sight the sun was fairly well up. The corralled animals whinnied. Hezekiah rode over and flung the gate open, Gus and Doug kept the cattle moving.

Dust arose, cattle ambled, the horses drifted, never very close, just close enough to keep the drive in sight.

The way they had first arrived on the huge mesa was by way of ancient game trails, which was the same way they drove the cattle. The trail was adequate but narrow; fortunately cattle were natural followers, but long before they got to the downward slope Hezekiah raised a gloved hand to point with.

There were two dust banners, one near the downward trail, another one coming due east in the direction of the drive.

As Hezekiah lowered his arm he said, "In'ians sure as hell," and he was right, but the tribesmen were not identifiable until they swept closer.

It was Gus who, after studying both dust banners, rode stirrup with Hezekiah and said, "They're cuttin' us off from the trail down out of here. Look yonder."

The first dust cloud had indeed reached the downward trail. Hezekiah spat, yanked his hat low and squinted.

Gus spoke again. "They got us cut off. My guess is that they ain't goin' to let us leave."

Hezekiah replied tartly, "First they want us off their mesa, then they don't . . . can you make out the stringbean one or Black Thunder?"

Gus loped toward the head of the drive. Up there the animals were following a well-marked trail and didn't need a rider to show the way.

Hezekiah stood in his stirrups which offered no particular advantage. The second band was heading directly for the middle of the drive. Hezekiah let go with a hair-raising curse. If the Indians rode into the middle of the strung-out herd cattle would stampede in every direction.

Hezekiah understood this as he swore and at the same time hooked his mount to intercept the Indians. Gus followed.

There was a considerable distance between the herd and the oncoming Indians. Hezekiah and Gus loped to make the interception, right hands high, palm forward.

When it was possible to make out individual Crows Hezekiah yelled at Gus. "They ain't goin' to stop!"

He was right. Four mounted Crows dropped to a slow lope but the others veered off to the right and left of the cowmen.

The four approaching Indians dropped

to a walk with hands raised. Hezekiah lowered his arm and rested the gloved hand atop the saddlehorn. Gus twisted to watch the other Crows come together behind him and drive straight for the middle of the cattle.

Gus sat forward. He recognised Black Thunder and the tall bronco called Squawman. The Indians were armed to the teeth. Squawman pushed ahead until he was close enough, then addressed Hezekiah. "Black Thunder say you stay."

Hezekiah glared. "First he wants us to leave, now he wants us to stay. Don't make sense."

Black Thunder drew rein beside the tall bronco. He gestured with his left arm pointing northward. "Boy say big bellies coming."

Hezekiah continued to glare. "That's why we're leavin'. It's one hell of a big bunch."

Black Thunder growled and his lanky companion interpreted, "You stay. Big bellies want meat."

Gus said, "Ahhh. You figure they'll kill our cattle an' maybe not fight you."

Squawman's attention shifted to Crandal. "No, we want them to see the cattle. They will scout up our camp, but cattle mean white men. They will want the meat first, fight us afterwards."

Hezekiah's sarcasm was obvious even to the Crows when he said, "You use my cattle to draw 'em away from your camp." Hezekiah leaned aside to expectorate before continuing. "Mister, we ain't interested in In'ians. I already told you that. Right now we're interested in getting us an' the cattle down off this mesa. If there's to be an In'ian fight, we figure to be a long way off when it happens."

Behind the cowmen mounted Indians rode into the strung-out cattle. Predictably, Hezekiah's animals put their tails in the air like scorpions and bolted. There was no particular direction to their panicked flight, some even went down the trail in the direction they were being driven. Those animals were turned back by Crow riders strung out to block the trail.

Hezekiah twisted to look back then sat forward mad as a hornet. He addressed Black Thunder. "You wanted us to leave an' we're leavin'. Then when Johnny told you how close them other In'ians is, you connivin' old bastard, you figured to use us and the cattle to divert the big bellies. For a plugged *centavo* I'd blow your head off!"

Whether Black Thunder understood all this was problematical but his companion understood and spoke sharply to Hezekiah. "We came to fight. You first if we got to for the cattle to stay here. Big bellies hate whites more than we do. If they get hold of you you won't die for two, three days."

Black Thunder signalled for his companion to stop talking. He looked steadily at big-bearded Hezekiah Strong when he spoke loudly, the noise of barking horsemen and bawling cattle was loud.

"You stay. You fight, or we tie you an' put you out where the big bellies can see you."

Somewhere amid the noise and dust back along the trail someone fired a gun. The palaverers looked back. The gunshot had been fired by Doug trying to turn cattle northward. It worked, a rawboned, slab-sided big cow with four feet of horn on each side of her head, bawled as she led other cattle, tongues lolling, wild eyed, stampeding as though their lives depended on it.

Hezekiah spat, straightened forward and addressed Black Thunder. "I hope you got a cache of sound money, In'ian, because as sure as I'm settin' this horse you're goin' to pay for every animal I lose."

Gus was silently watching horse-Indians beginning to return to the place the palavering was taking place. He counted over forty. He spoke to Hezekiah. "Let's get back; gettin' the cattle settled'll take the rest of the day, and gawd knows where the horses is." Gus gestured with his rein-hand. "Hezekiah, there's a pile of armed tomahawks. They ain't goin' to let us leave the mesa, so let's get back."

Squawman eyed Gus sombrely. In his experience he had encountered few whites worth their salt, but the bronzed, hard-eyed man who had just spoken was *coyote*. Squawman said something to Black Thunder and reined around. The converging Indians gazed at the Texans as they followed their spokesman.

Hezekiah jettisoned his cud and said, "That old son of a bitchin' warwhoop!"

Gus said nothing, just turned to help drift the cattle back the way they had come. A solitary rider appeared in the distance. He passed the Indians at a lope heading toward Hezekiah and Gus. When he reached them he said, "There was nothin' I could do. After I told 'em how close them other In'ians is, they left me with two old men, got a-horseback and left in a rush."

Hezekiah, who had never had children and who sort of fathered Johnny Tremaine, despite his anger, said, "You done right. That old bastard just outsmarted us."

As Gus had opined, it required the rest of daylight to get the cattle settled and even then there were critters who did not get over being spooked. They would bolt if a rider got too close, but they paralleled the driven critters back to good feed and creek water.

It was dusk before tired men and tired horses got back to the yard. They used creek water to wash their horses' backs, went to the log house, fired up some candles and passed the jug. There was little talk, they hadn't eaten since before daylight. Doug Hardy was an experienced camp cook. He did not like the job but after a few meals made by the others he assumed the role as cook.

After supper with dusk fading into night they went outside to the bench, some lighted quirlies but the chewers tucked molasses-cured into their cheeks.

The corralled horses were not too tired to be hungry. They would get nothing to eat until the following morning when they were turned out. Hezekiah said, "That sly old rascal. He got us set up."

Doug Hardy had been thinking of what he and Gus had discussed earlier out at the corral. "Suppose we snuck up where them big bellies set up camp and fired the countryside."

For a long moment there was silence, then Hezekiah spoke. "It's an idea. We ain't got a lot of time to do it an' sure as hell they'll have scouts out."

Doug persisted. "They always got scouts out. The thing is, do they know them Crows is at the far end of the mesa? Likely they know it by now, which means they'll be real careful. But it's a gamble, an' settin' here ponderin' ain't goin' to do us any good."

Hezekiah was quiet long enough for Johnny Tremaine to speak. "It'd scatter 'em sure as hell. But I'm wonderin' — the Crows know they're comin'. They might be plannin' somethin' like maybe attackin' first, which might put us between the Crows an' the big bellies."

Hezekiah shot up to his feet. He studied the sky briefly before wagging his head. "Trouble. All we run into since startin' out is trouble."

Gus made a point. "It's one thing to have settled cowmen run us off an' somethin' different to get into an In'ian war. But we're in it, like it or not. Whatever the Crows figure to do, it can't hurt if we try somethin' too — like a big fire near the camp of the big bellies."

Hezekiah gravely nodded, although he was dog-tired and would have liked nothing better than to climb into his soogans. He said, "The horses ain't in real good shape." When no one offered a contradiction, Hezekiah also said, "How far'd they be in camp, Gus?"

Crandal had no idea but from what he had seen of the slow-moving straggle of Indians he thought they couldn't be more than maybe twelve or fifteen miles distant. "The way they been travellin' I'd guess they won't get close until sometime tomorrow."

It was a reasonable guess except for one thing: If big belly scouts had seen the mesa with smoke rising from Crow tipis, the hostiles would possibly be much closer.

Johnny Tremaine arose watching Hezekiah, who was looking in the direction of the corral when he said, "We'll favour the horses as much as we can." Hezekiah yawned and reached inside his shirt to scratch.

When they were rigged out and ready to ride, each man with a laden saddle boot and a loaded Colt suspended from a shell belt with few empty loops, Hezekiah motioned for Gus to take the lead. The reason he did this was because he hadn't been able to see well at night for the last couple of years, also because Gus could back-track the trail they had used to return from their earlier exploratory ride. Gus was a good sign reader.

There was a moon, a sort of sickly, swollen crescent, which was better than no moon. Otherwise the sky was cloudless and speckled with more diamond-chip stars than a man could count in several lifetimes.

Johnny Tremaine, imbued with the resilience of youth, did not slouch in the saddle as the older men were doing. He and Doug Hardy rode stirrup where the trail permitted and although Johnny wanted to talk the lack of response from Hardy eventually made him silent.

They encountered scattered bands of bedded cattle, who sprang to their feet at the sound of riders. Some pawed and rattled their horns but the riders scarcely noticed as they passed.

They left the mesa a few miles northward. From here on the territory was timbered, brushy, rocky and in places steep enough to make their animals tread warily. The only sound was of dislodged rocks rattling into canyons.

Eventually Gus halted peering ahead. When the others came up he pointed. Distantly the sullen glare of dying fires showed clearly. Hezekiah leaned on his saddlehorn. "Closer'n I figured, Gus."

Crandal's reply was dry. "They know about the Crows sure as hell otherwise they wouldn't have pushed ahead the way they had to do to be this close."

Doug dryly commented, "If they're this close I'd guess the Crows scouted 'em up. Nothin' like bein' caught between Hell an' a hot place."

Hezekiah scratched inside his shirt again while peering at the distant dying fires. "How far, Gus?"

"Mile. Maybe two miles."

"Ride on a ways, find a place to leave the horses."

Gus nodded, but as he moved ahead the hair on the back of his neck was stiffening. As sure as Gawd had made green apples the big bellies would have scouts out and sentinels around their camp. He did not ride very far. Where he halted and swung off there was a tiny clearing, no more than two acres. The land was fairly flat. Without looking around he selected a tree with low limbs, made his horse fast, slipped the Winchester from its boot and waited until the others had done the same. As they were moving ahead on foot Hezekiah growled at Johnny, "Take them damned spurs off!"

Tremaine obeyed sheepishly. He had acquired a pair of Chihuahua spurs with rowels as large as the palm of a man's hand some years earlier. He had liked the sound they made when he walked through dirt and dust. He looped them over a spindly limb and joined the others in their quiet stalk.

The terrain was ruggedly timbered, rocky, with occasional patches of buckbrush and thornpin in rare clearings. Mostly, they climbed up hillsides, descended on the far side then had to climb again. Gus was of the opinion that if the big bellies had scouts out they would also be afoot. This was not good horseback country.

Eventually they caught the scent of wood smoke, faint but recognisable.

The sky shed very little light through stiff-topped pine and fir trees. The advantage was that the ground was spongy with layers of pine and fir needles. They made no noise as they passed along.

When smoke-scent was strong Gus held up his hand for the others to wait, and went ahead holding his saddle gun in both hands.

Hezekiah got a fresh cud tucked into his cheek and looked around. Johnny Tremaine hadn't said a word since before they'd left the horses. Hezekiah made a small, hard smile. He knew how it was when someone was young — and scairt peeless. He'd had the identical experience many times when he'd been Johnny's age.

Gus was gone a long time. It troubled

Doug who whispered to Hezekiah and left in the direction Gus had taken. Johnny came up to Hezekiah and loudly whispered. "Can you smell In'ians? I knew an old buffler hunter who said he could."

Hezekiah was worrying so his answer was curt. "Texas Comanches got a rank smell. These In'ians maybe don't smell. Don't talk, Johnny."

Doug returned carrying two Winchesters. One belonged to him the other one belonged to Gus Crandal. Hezekiah growled. "Lead us to where you found it."

Doug leaned the spare saddle gun against a tree and faced Hezekiah. "They're around us," he said.

Hezekiah woodenly nodded. "Take us to where you found Gus's gun!"

Doug led off but there was no mistaking his wariness even in the poor light. Johnny brought up the rear, head moving constantly, Winchester held across his middle with both hands. One finger was curled inside the trigger guard, the thumb of the other hand was atop the hammer. He was as wary as a cougar, did not allow Hezekiah to get more than eight or ten feet ahead.

Where Doug finally halted and pointed, it was impossible to make out whether there had been a struggle or not. Hezekiah did not believe there had been. He thought someone had clubbed Gus from behind but he did not mention this. In fact he did not speak at all until Doug gasped. He was staring behind Hezekiah.

There was no sign of Johnny!

Hezekiah turned slowly from side to side and behind. Doug came up to whisper what he'd said earlier. "They're all around."

Hezekiah ignored both his companion and the statement. He cocked his carbine and went soundlessly westerly among huge old overripe fir trees. Doug followed but only because he preferred not being alone.

Hezekiah abruptly disappeared in a flourishing buckbrush thicket. When

Doug was close enough he reached out with a powerful hand and yanked Doug so hard Hardy fell. Hezekiah stilled a curse. Doug had rattled the buckbrush when he had fallen.

Hezekiah hunched his massive body well below the tallest limbs of their hiding place. Doug did the same. He was scarcely breathing.

Nothing happened. After a tense long wait Hezekiah twisted to see behind. It was too dark to discern anything but trees and underbrush. There was neither movement nor a man-like silhouette.

Doug's grip on Hezekiah's forearm brought the larger and older man around. Doug did not point nor make a sound. He did not have to. It wasn't one Indian it was three of them, two spread far on each side of the third one who was moving to sidestep the big stand of buckbrush.

There was an excellent chance the sidestepping bronco would not look to his left and discern the crouching white men, but Hezekiah had no illusions. He may not have known much about upland Indians but the ones he did know, Texas and New Mexico Indians, had eyes in the backs of their heads.

He touched Doug and began sidling a few inches at a time to the south. If there hadn't been needles to make this kind of movement soundless, as well as very poor light, they might not have been able to sidle as far as they did before Doug touched Hezekiah and jutted his jaw Indian-fashion. One of the broncos, the one who had fanned out southward was now also stalking westerly. He would come within about thirty feet of the sweating Texans.

The Indian behind them was already passing soundlessly beyond their hiding place, leaning slightly, like a stalking cougar, concentrating his attention on the dark forest westward. From this bronco Hezekiah and Doug were fairly safe. It was the Indian passing by southward who kept his head moving, who posed the real threat.

They could not hide in the buckbrush. Any movement, even the quivering limbs of underbrush would be noticed by the man southward who did not concentrate ahead, but warily watched while peering from side to side.

Hezekiah measured the distance. When the Indian sidestepped a forest giant and an ancient lichen-covered boulder he was less than fifteen feet from Hezekiah whose legs were as taut as steel springs.

The moment he launched himself the Indian saw him and twisted to bring his Winchester to bear — too late. Over two hundred pounds of hurtling bearded human projectile knocked the Indian over the boulder where he flailed to stop his fall and lost the carbine.

He had no time to use his fleshing knife. Hezekiah pinned him over the old rock, blocked a cry with his right forearm across the Indian's gullet and swung his ham-sized fist. The sound of the blow carried. The Indian turned slack. Hezekiah let him slide off the boulder, yanked the big knife from its holster and hissed for Doug to follow him.

The noise they made brought barking yelps from the remaining Indians who rushed in pursuit, not of wraiths they could not see but the sounds of fleeing men.

Hezekiah ran blind, avoiding trees, brush and boulders right up until several Indians appeared to block his passage with raised weapons.

Hezekiah halted breathing like a fish out of water. Doug stopped at his side.

5

Taking the Initiative

THE Indians blocking the path did not fire. They stood like dark statues, Winchesters snugged against brawny shoulders.

One Indian; taller than the others and lean, gradually lowered his Winchester. Behind him a warrior snarled something in their language and the tall bronco spoke. "You come to warn the big bellies; lead them back to our camp."

It wasn't a question it was a statement made in a knife-edged tone of voice.

Hezekiah loosened while regarding the tall Indian. "We come to keep them from reachin' the mesa."

"How?" Squawman asked.

"Set fires along the way they got to go to reach the mesa."

Behind the tall Indian that same snarling man spoke again, but not in English. Squawman listened and nodded slightly before speaking. "Black Thunder don't believe you."

Hezekiah's retort was blunt. "To hell with Black Thunder. How many In'ians with you?"

"Enough to sneak up closer and shoot into the camp."

Hezekiah shook his head. "No. You'n us got to fan out an' set fires. They'll burn hot this time of year. Got to set 'em all along the trail them big bellies got to take to reach the mesa." Hezekiah moved sideways in order to see Black Thunder. "You got plenty of flints?"

Black Thunder did not answer, he inclined his head.

"Then scatter your lads. Not too far apart. Tell 'em to set fires."

Squawman spoke in Crow to the spokesman and Black Thunder dryly replied in English. "Why you take our side?"

Hezekiah's reply was blunt. "To save my cattle."

Black Thunder stood exchanging a long look with Hezekiah before speaking in Crow to Squawman. The tall Indian moved swiftly and soundlessly among the warriors, most of whom neither of the Texans had seen. Black Thunder then addressed Hezekiah and Gus in English. "You go back now."

Hezekiah stood wide-legged and obdurate. "Not on your damned life. We stay."

Squawman returned, spoke swiftly to Black Thunder after which the older Crow again used English. "We got three big belly scouts. Come along."

How the capture had been accomplished neither Hezekiah nor Doug ever knew, but one, a burly Indian with a knife scar across his nose was unsteady from a blow. He sat down, the other captives did the same.

A dark captive with a broad nose considered the pair of Texans and spoke. "If we catch you we'll cook you."

Hezekiah considered the Crow captors around the big bellies, and mirthlessly smiled. "Only thing your folks is goin' to catch is somethin' hot as hell. How many people with your party?"

The scar-faced Indian lied with a clear conscience. "Three hunnert warriors. Six hunnert others."

Squawman snorted and Black Thunder drew his knife and leaned. When the blade touched the scarfaced man's throat he said, "Seventy warriors."

Black Thunder sheathed the knife, looked at Squawman and spoke in Crow. Squawman answered in English. "No full-blood. Half-black soldier."

A youngster whom Hezekiah recognised came out of the night to say the Crow bucks were ready to start fires. He also said the big bellies' loose stock was in a clearing north of the bivouac and appeared to be awaiting what either the tall man or Black Thunder would say. It was not a very long wait. Black Thunder used English. "No! You try goin' around the camp too unlucky. Go with the others, they'll tell you what to do."

Before the young man departed he cast a quizzical look at the pair of Texans.

Hezekiah was getting impatient. He held his gun in the crook of one arm and nodded to the Indians. He led the way back in the direction of their earlier flight. For the first time in an hour Doug spoke. "Them broncos we hid from was Crows?"

"Seems so."

"Well, you pretty well larruped the hell out of that one you knocked across the boulder."

"Couldn't be helped." Hezekiah began bearing westerly. He unexpectedly encountered Gus and Johnny Tremaine. They stepped out of the gloom from behind huge old trees. Hezekiah did not address either Crandal or Tremaine, he jerked his head for them to follow and quickened his step as the faint scent of smoke became discernible from behind them westerly.

They paused occasionally to gather kindling and set small fires. Smoke scent increased. Occasionally as the Texans moved westerly they caught sight of fires behind them, but it was a long time before big bellies in their camp became alarmed and raised the yell.

Hezekiah stood south of the last fire they started listening to the increasing racket from the camp which he could not see. Had it been daylight he might not have been able to see the camp either. Between ancient trees, stands of brush taller than a man and boulders, visibility was limited to only a few feet, but the noise from the rousing camp northward told Hezekiah all he had to know.

He was turning to address Johnny when a solitary rifle shot sounded in the near distance. Tremaine went down like a pole-axed steer. Doug and Gus scattered in the direction from which the shot had come. Hezekiah knelt beside young Tremaine. It was difficult to locate the wound in the dark, but bloody fingers helped him find it. If the hostile who had fired had been aiming for Johnny's head — a poor target even in broad daylight — he hadn't missed by much. The slug had torn across Tremaine's shoulder up high and close to the neck. It had also, for some reason, slanted abruptly upwards raking a sliver of scalp.

Hezekiah used the youth's own bandanna to staunch the blood. In short order it was soaked through. Someone appeared without sound, stood a long moment without moving then approached and dropped to one knee and grunted. Hezekiah turned. He had never cared much for the spokesman and right now his glare was cold as he prepared to speak. Black Thunder put aside his Winchester, fished in his parfleche with one hand and with one sweep of the other hand got most of the blood clear of the head wound, and with the other hand slapped something directly over the injury. He looked at Hezekiah as he said, "Torn rag an' spider webs."

North of them the fire was coming together from east to west. It was growing enough to shed strange reddish light where the two older men hunkered beside the unconscious youth. The heat was increasing by the moment.

Black Thunder got both arms under young Tremaine and stood up. Hezekiah followed. Black Thunder did not stop and put Johnny down until they had travelled far enough south-west to feel no heat, just a slight chill which indicated the night was getting along toward dawn.

The Crow stood briefly gazing at the youth then abruptly turned and was soon lost in darkness.

Hezekiah was torn between remaining with Johnny Tremaine or going up where the fire was spreading to create an impenetrable wall between the camping Indians and any southward route. He was joined by a sweating Doug Hardy who knelt and studied the unconscious youth before saying, "They're yellin' an' runnin' around like a gang of sheep. We done all we set out to do, Hezekiah."

The larger man rocked back on both heels to listen. The sounds of the fire nearly precluded other sounds but an occasional yell reached him. He said, "Stay with him, Doug," and left.

The fire was reaching toward treetops. Because trees were close together there was no way for anyone from the north, or the south, to pass through.

Hezekiah met several Indians and eventually met the tall, lean one. Squawman was breathing hard and sweat-shiny in the reflected firelight. He said, "Their horses stampeded. They're goin' after 'em. Listen."

Dogs were barking, women were screaming, men were yelling. The wall of fire had succeeded in its purpose better than Hezekiah had expected.

There was an occasional gunshot but for the most part the big bellies were fleeing northward away from the spreading wall of flame, yelling in panic.

Hezekiah looked for Gus Crandal, failed to find him and was turning southward when a Gros Ventre hurled himself to the ground with clothing afire. There was a spongy carpet of dry pine and fir needles. His instinctive effort to roll on earth to kill the flames simply fired the dry needles as he rolled.

Hezekiah shot him. A quick death was preferable to a lingering one than to a human being burning like a torch.

He went to the thicket where he and Doug had hidden, found Crandal leaning against a forest mammoth watching the flames. Hezekiah gruffly said, "Let's go. We got to carry Johnny where we left the horses."

When they arrived where Doug was watching Johnny, Hezekiah did not hesitate. He picked up the youth and led off in the direction of their horses.

They were not there.

Hezekiah put Johnny down. Without

horses they were afoot many miles from the mesa. Gus growled something and turned back, angling left and right.

The flames had driven the Crows southward. Heat made the needles on living trees shrivel and droop. Several Crows passed southward like ghosts. One stopped at sight of Hezekiah. It was the youth named Long Walker. Hezekiah asked where Black Thunder was. Instead of answering Long Walker jerked his head and led off westerly. It was not a long walk. When he found the spokesman Gus had already explained about the missing horses. Black Thunder sent Squawman and three other warriors to find the horses. He did not say who had taken them, he did not have to. There were only Crows south of the fire.

By the time Hezekiah and Gus returned to Doug and Johnny, the youngest Texan was sitting propped against a tree, conscious but in excruciating pain. His clothing was bloody, somewhere during the fire-fight he had lost his saddle gun but still had his holstered Colt.

Squawman and a burly Crow appeared with their animals. Hezekiah and Squawman got Johnny atop his horse. Doug and Gus rode on each side to prevent a fall and Hezekiah led off back the way they had come.

There was still an occasional gunshot, but the Texans were eventually too far southward to hear much.

Behind them the world was orange-red. Ahead of them predawn was turning night into a sickly shade of grey.

They could smell smoke all the way back to Mandan Mesa. They could also still see the orange firelight above tall treetops.

They took Johnny inside to a bunk. Doug and Gus returned to care for the horses. While they were doing this Gus said, "My guess is that them big bellies'll figure out that fire didn't start itself an' when they're ready they'll come down here for blood."

94

Doug was sanguine. "If they come maybe the Crows'll lend a hand."

Gus was not convinced. "They want us out of here. If the big bellies do it the Crows won't have to."

They spent most of the night making Johnny comfortable. They got enough popskull down him to float a small boat and could not be sure the whiskey had numbed the pain because Johnny fell asleep with a bandage around his head as big as a turban. The shoulder wound would heal in time. There would be an indentation and a scar, negligible things, hardly a frontiersman did not have something similar.

The following morning Doug and Gus went to the creek to have an all-over bath while Hezekiah fussed over Johnny, whose headache was not as bad as it had been but it still prevented Tremaine from moving his head quickly.

Hezekiah went to the creek to also bathe while Doug went about rassling a meal. None of them had eaten in a long while. Doug could have served up roast rattlesnake and they would have devoured it down to the rattles.

Northward the fire was still raging and would continue to do so until it rained or until the flames came to a barren place with nothing for them to feed on.

The smoke came southward on a light breeze, it hindered visibility. Hezekiah and Doug went looking for the cattle. Gus made a cold compress for Johnny's head fresh from the creek, which seemed to do more for the youngest Texan than anything else. Along toward evening the headache dwindled and Johnny slept. Gus took his blood-stiff britches and butternut shirt to the creek and beat them unmercifully on rocks. He was draping them to dry when Doug and Hezekiah returned. They had found most of the hundred head. The ones they did not find wouldn't be far from the main herd. Cattle might not be the smartest animals on the hoof but they had one characteristic which made handling them easier than it would have been otherwise, they tended to gang together, keep one another in sight.

That evening the pall of smoke diminished and there was no longer an angry orange glare along the northerly skyline. Gus guessed the fire had burned itself out for lack of anything to keep it alive.

Johnny slept through supper. The others conversed sporadically. Hezekiah was the least talkative. Once, between mouthfuls he glared. "That old son of a bitch said we was tryin' to lead them hostiles to his camp."

From the mud-stone stove Doug replied, "If you was suspicious of someone an' seen 'em close to your enemies, what would you figure?"

The topic ended there, until supper was past and they were outside on the bench, then Gus made a remark that did not set well with the others.

"You reckon them big bellies'll come together somewhere an' come back to settle the score? They sure as hell know where the mesa is, an' more'n likely they know where the Crow rancheria is."

Hezekiah put a sour look on Crandal. "Gus, in all the time we been together I can't recollect you ever seein' the bright side of things."

Gus gazed dispassionately at Hezekiah. "The difference between us is that you look into the future ridin' your butt raw lookin' for a place to settle an' raise a herd. Me, I don't worry about the future, it's got a way of takin' care of itself, for better or worse. I figure life from day to day, an' right now I think we're likely to be in more trouble with them hostile In'ians than we ever was with Black Thunder's people."

It was a long statement for Crandal, who ordinarily did not put his anxieties into words. Hezekiah was silent long enough for Doug to put in his two bits worth. "Seems to me no matter where folks settle — find some place they like better'n any other place they been — fate or somethin' crops up with obstacles. I ain't sure the Crows are grateful for us figurin' ways to scatter their enemies, but I got to agree with Gus. Ol' Jim Bridger put it about right when he said, if you don't kill the nits they'll grow into lice. We scattered them big bellies, but they got to be real Christian In'ians not to come huntin' us an' the Crows for revenge."

Johnny coughing in the cabin brought Hezekiah to his feet. After his departure Doug Hardy said, "Gus, we're settin' ducks. Bein' In'ians them hostiles'll scout us up real good, an' if there's enough of 'em, fortin' up in the house won't do more'n delay a massacre."

Crandal pouched a chew into his cheek and spat once before saying, "That's a boot that fits both feet. You'n me done our share of skulkin'."

Doug understood the implication, pondered a moment then spoke. "Just ahead of first light, Gus. Hezekiah can mind Johnny."

They went inside where four candles

made adequate light.

Johnny was feverish. Hezekiah had placed a water-soaked cloth over his forehead. When Gus and Doug approached Johnny's cot Hezekiah said, "He seemed to be on the mend," and paused to look at the wounded Texan on his bunk. "I'd give ten cows to know who shot him."

Gus leaned to feel Johnny's face; it was hot to the touch, visibly flushed and sweaty even by candle light. He straightened back without speaking. Folks died of infection. Johnny seemed to have the symptoms.

The whiskey jug was handy. Gus swallowed twice, replaced the jug and saw both Hardy and Hezekiah gazing at him. Hezekiah growled, "He's goin' to make it. He's got to make it . . . In'ians! Even the tame ones is trouble."

Doug was less passionate. "That town we passed some weeks ago, the sign said Hartstrand. They likely got a doctor. They got an army post down there. Soldiers always got a doctor."

Hezekiah snorted. "That damned town's sixty miles from here. Gettin' the lad down there'd kill him."

Doug's answer drove his companions into silence. "I didn't mean take him down there, I meant for one of us to go find the doctor and bring him up here."

Gus returned to the jug for another couple of swallows. As certain as sunrise the hostiles they had burnt out would have eyes everywhere. One horseman leaving the mesa would end up looking like a pincushion.

Gus shoved the jug away and sank down at the table. He was quiet so long Doug and Hezekiah seemed to forget him as they leaned over the copiously sweating, delirious youth.

Gus finally spoke. "I don't know what them Crows know, but sure as hell they've had folks shot up." Gus gazed at the flushed youth whose breathing was gusty. "None of us know about patchin' him up."

Hezekiah interrupted. "You mean

go over yonder and fetch back their medicine man?" Hezekiah snorted. "All they do is shake rattles an' holler an' dance."

Gus did not relent. "That's more'n we know. Hezekiah, the lad's real bad off." He arose, dropped his hat on the back of his head and said, "I'll go over there. You keep him alive until I get back."

Nothing was said until Gus had closed the door after himself, then Hezekiah also went to pull on the jug before returning to the stool beside the cot. As he gazed at Johnny Tremaine he softly said, "Gawdamned In'ians."

Doug went to sit at the table. He ignored the jug, gazed at the delirious youth and said, "Likely nothin' will come of it, but them tomahawks owe us, an' there's nothin' else we can do."

Hezekiah went out into the night to soak the cloth in cold creek water. As he stood looking at the star-spattered sky he made an imploring prayer, something he hadn't done in fifty years.

6

Bad Signs

IT was a long ride and a bad night, the wind which had been blowing from the south had switched around and was now blowing from the north. It carried clouds of acrid-scented smoke.

Hezekiah removed the bandages, rinsed them clean and used his only other shirt, which was as clean as beating it on the rocks at the creek could make it. When he was ready to do the re-bandaging Doug came to lean and look. The shoulder wound looked normal but the gash up alongside the head was swollen and red. Doug said, "Don't look good."

Hezekiah hurled a fierce look at Doug. "It'll mend," he snarled and Doug retreated to the bench out front.

The smoke was like a thick fog. He

could barely make out the corral. He fell asleep, legs outstretched, shoulders against logs. What awakened him was the sound of riders whose advent was greeted by whinnying from the corral. He stepped inside to alert Hezekiah, took his saddle gun with him and returned to the porch.

Gus sang out before Doug could make him out. Hezekiah came to the doorway holding a soggy bit of cloth. Satisfied who the riders were he went back inside to Johnny Tremaine's bedside.

Gus had three Indians with him. The youngest was Long Walker, Johnny's Crow friend. Another was Squawman, recognisable by his height. The third was an old Indian, wizened, as wiry as a monkey with sunk-set dark eyes with muddy whites. He carried an army saddle with him as he and Squawman approached the log house, leaving Long Walker to tend the saddle stock.

The old man did not speak a word of English, nor did he smile when they met Doug holding his Winchester. Squawman made a curt greeting before introducing the old man as Running Dog, what the Mexicans called a *curandero*. The old man, Squawman explained, had been captured by Mexicans as a child, had grown up among them as one of their own and had learned many secrets of healing from them.

Doug listened to all this without realising Hezekiah was again in the doorway until he said, "Come inside," addressing the old man and his tall companion.

The old man called for all four candles to be set close then made a meticulous and unhurried examination of Johnny Tremaine.

Doug came inside but remained beyond reach of candlelight as he watched the old bronco rummage in his saddlebag. What he drew forth was a long object with a sharpened point. He spoke to Squawman in their language. Squawman brushed Hezekiah

105

aside, leaned and held Johnny's head with both hands. The old man leaned, pushed cloth and hair clear and with a movement almost too quick to be noticed, lanced the largest swelling.

The bad-smelling effusion which flowed from the fresh wound the old man caught in a rag. He worked as much from the puncture as he could, turned and handed the rag to Hezekiah.

His movements were slow. He only moved quickly when Johnny abruptly fought to sit up. Hezekiah dropped the rag on the table and joined Squawman in holding the youth down. Johnny was conscious. He saw the wrinkled old Indian leaning over him with the sharp lances in one hand and called for help. Hezekiah spoke gently, which had no effect. Johnny was still struggling when Running Dog leaned, placed two gnarled fingers on Johnny's neck, one on each side, and young Tremaine turned slack and fell back.

Long Walker entered, pushed past

Doug to join the other Indians at bedside. He said something in Crow which Squawman answered curtly. "No. He's not dead . . . you are in the light."

Running Dog, his full attention on Johnny, looked at the shoulder wound, made a low grunt and put the lancing instrument back in his saddle-bag. He then brought forth a small buckskin pouch, worked the lanced wound until only blood came, and as he put several pinches of powder from the little bag on the wound he spoke to Squawman.

The tall Indian faced Hezekiah. "He said he leave little bag. Every morning you wash wound, sprinkle some powder on it."

Hezekiah nodded. "Will he be all right?"

Squawman and Running Dog spoke briefly before the tall Crow faced Hezekiah again. "Maybe. Maybe not. Old man say he has bad blood. If it is inside his body he will die. He don't know if he has bad blood inside. He say for you to use the powder every day, give him plenty of water. Wash him, he stinks."

Doug came into the light to consider Johnny Tremaine. He asked Squawman a question. "What's the powder from the little pouch?"

Squawman and Running Dog again conversed briefly while the old man stood looking steadily at Johnny Tremaine, who was regaining consciousness. Squawman said, "Running Dog won't tell what the powder is. He goes away to make it. It comes from a swampy place."

Doug went to fire up the stove and make coffee. Squawman drank some but the old man shook his head. To him coffee was the colour of death and had a bad taste. He went out to the creek to kneel and wash his hands. When he returned Long Walker caught him and asked the same question Hezekiah had asked. This time Running Dog's reply was curt. "No. Not with bad blood."

Hezekiah offered silver to the old

man, who eyed it dispassionately. He had lived a long time, he knew what money was. He also knew he had no use for a piece of silver. It was too soft even to be melted into musket balls. He declined with a shake of the head, looked enquiringly at Squawman and went out where his horse was hobbled.

Squawman could add nothing to what the old man had already said. He too left the cabin. Long Walker had already removed the hobbles of both their animals.

Doug and Gus watched the Indians until poor visibility and darkness hid them. Gus sank down on the bench. He had something to say that he hadn't said inside while Running Dog was working on Johnny, but when Doug eased down beside him Gus said, "They had six captives."

Doug looked at Gus. "They killed 'em?"

"Yep. They're worryin' about somethin' else. They got scouts out all around.

Big bellies got scattered pretty bad but there's a war party comin' toward the mesa."

Doug was too tired to worry, he said Gus should tell Hezekiah. If a war party was gathering, they might still have time to get down off the mesa.

Gus looked at Doug. "You forgot them Crows'll keep us here?"

Hezekiah appeared in the doorway, he was holding the whiskey jug. He came to the bench, sank down and held out the jug. As Doug took it Gus said again what he had learned at the Crow camp. Hezekiah leaned back and thrust his legs out. His reaction was less than either of his companions expected. Eventually he said, "That old shrivelled In'ian didn't look to me like he figured Johnny would make it."

Gus replied quietly, he as well as Doug knew how Hezekiah felt toward Johnny, the son he had never had and never would have. "He got a lot of poison out, Hezekiah. I've cut galls on horses with distemper. It smells awful

110

and looked like what was in Johnny. None of 'em ever died."

Hezekiah took back the jug, put it between his feet and looked around. "Did you say a big belly war party's comin'?"

"That's what they told me at the rancheria," Gus replied.

"It figures," Hezekiah stated. "How big a party?"

Gus did not know. "Crow scouts seen 'em comin' together north-east. All Black Thunder knew was that it was a war party."

Hezekiah thought a moment before speaking again. "From the size of that camp I'd guess it's maybe big enough. Is Black Thunder gettin' ready?"

All Gus could say about that was that the Crows were holding a council. Hezekiah's response was laconic. "At least they ain't fixin' to strike camp an' run for it like In'ians in other places."

Gus was silent. Hezekiah had seen the Crow camp. It was a permanent one, the kind folks where he had come from called a *rancheria*, a permanent camp.

Doug asked about Johnny. "Sleepin' like a log," Hezekiah replied and as though reminded of something arose and went back inside.

Gus stood up and stretched while gazing in the direction of the corral. "In'ians or not we got to graze the horses in the mornin'," and went inside to kick out of his boots, dump his hat on the floor and roll his gun and shellbelt before dropping on his bunk. Within moments he was asleep.

The following morning before sunrise Doug and Gus were at the creek. They could hear Hezekiah snoring even at that distance. Doug said, "Sat up most of the night with Johnny." He was towering when he also said, "That place the old bronco lanced is sore again. Likely full of pus again."

Inside, Doug went about preparing breakfast. The scent of smoke still lingered but visibility had improved and by sunrise would improve still more.

Johnny was lying full length with both eyes open mumbling things neither Gus nor Doug could understand. Gus went to stand by the bunk, was still standing there looking down when Hezekiah sat up, rubbed his eyes, scratched and dressed. He saw the way Gus was standing and hurriedly stamped into his boots, crossed the room and also stared. Johnny's gaze was fixed straight ahead. He did not see them at bedside. He began his incomprehensible babbling again. Hezekiah saw the fresh swelling. "We got to drain it," he said, and fumbled in a trouser pocket for his clasp knife. Before he could lean Gus said, "Dip the blade in hot water, Hezekiah." It was sound advice, the blade was brown and sticky from being used to skive chewing tobacco.

Doug removed the lid from the coffee water for Hezekiah to immerse the blade. Afterward he gave Hezekiah a rag to wipe the blade with. It was clean and sharp.

This time, since none of them knew how Running Dog had made Johnny briefly unconscious, the youth struggled, swore and reacted as though he was fighting for his life, which in his delirious condition he probably believed he was.

He was naturally strong and while Hardy who was larger and also strong, had a real fight of it in his effort to keep Johnny from breaking away.

Gus came over, gripped Johnny's head on both sides until Hezekiah made the cut. Johnny fainted. Doug returned to his cooking. Gus used a scrap of paper to catch the poison and Hezekiah went to the creek to soak a rag in cold water.

When he returned Gus had placed the soggy paper on the table. Along with pus there was blood.

Hezekiah fixed the cold cloth over Johnny's forehead and sat on the edge of the bunk as he spoke to no one in particular. "How many times is he goin' to get that build-up? Inside he must be makin' that stuff no matter how often we let it out."

Doug spoke from the cooking area. "Douse the wound with some of that powder the old In'ian gave you."

Hezekiah obeyed and whether the powder had anything to do with it or not, Johnny subsided, breathing raggedly and showing sweat on his upper lip. It wasn't that warm in the cabin, it surely wasn't that warm outside with the sun just beginning its daylong climb.

Doug took the horses out to graze. While they were doing that he rode elsewhere looking for cattle. He eventually found most of them. Most importantly he had located the three bulls — standing together in a muddy place getting rid of the fever too much hot, gritty soil had caused their feet.

As he was riding back to the horses he saw an Indian watching him from a barren upthrust. The distance was considerable but Doug felt sure this tomahawk did not roach his hair, which meant he was not a Crow.

He headed the horses for the corral, sidled into a deep gully, left his horse tied, took his Winchester and sneaked back up the arroyo until he came to some cottonwood trees. There, he climbed high enough to be able to see out of the gully.

The Indian was gone.

He got back down, retrieved his mount, came up out of the arroyo and allowed the loose stock another hour of cropping feed until he drove them slowly in the direction of the yard. They grazed along as they went. By the time he corralled them their hunger had been satisfied, although they had not been grazed long enough. The custom was to let the horses graze all day and corral them at night.

Hezekiah and Gus listened in stony silence to what Doug reported. It surprised neither of them that they were being scouted up, although they had thought the Crow village would be the first objective of hostiles.

They discussed warning the Crows but Gus was of the opinion that whether Crow scouts had seen that particular hostile, if the war party was scouting up the mesa, Crow scouts would know about it.

Hezekiah tended Johnny Tremaine. Doug and Gus exchanged a knowing look. The possibility of an imminent attack took second place in the big, bearded man's thoughts.

In late afternoon while Gus was beating his clothing on rocks at the creek a cock pheasant loudly crowed.

There was a variety of birds on Mandan Mesa but no pheasants. Gus left his wet wash on a rock and stood up. The pheasant crowed again. The sound was coming from the vicinity of a spit of young oaks north and west. Gus could see beyond the trees and also to the east and west. There were not even any cattle in sight.

He left his clothing where he had dropped them and walked briskly to the cabin. Inside, he told Hezekiah what had happened, got his Winchester and went back outside where shade from the overhang fairly well concealed him.

Doug came out with his saddle gun, ignored Gus, went to the south side of the structure and was gone from sight in moments.

It was a long wait. Eventually Hezekiah got his carbine and moved close to Gus in porch shade. There was another pheasant call, otherwise there was nothing, no movement, no sound, just miles of sunbaked summer countryside.

Gus said, "If it's them hostiles they must want the cattle more 'n they want the Crows."

Doug returned from his reconnaissance southward and westerly. He had seen nothing, and he had a suggestion to offer. "I never seen or heard pheasants up here, but that don't mean there ain't any."

An hour passed, Hezekiah went back inside, Gus and Doug waited and watched. Gus made a dry comment. "We'd be settin' ducks shade or no shade, if there was trees or brush for 'em to get within gun range."

Doug sat down, leaned his weapon aside and rolled a quirly. As he trickled smoke he said, "I been in some tight places in my life but damned if I was before caught between two bunches of In'ians, one in front, one behind that don't want us to leave."

The cock pheasant crowed again, this time somewhere closer than the bosque of oaks. Both Texans narrowed their eyes. Doug softly said, "He's somewhere easterly, usin' the corral an' the horses for cover."

Very abruptly someone called loudly enough for Hezekiah to hear the sound inside the cabin. "Long Walker! Long Walker!"

Doug swore a blue streak. "Get up where we can see you — you clanged idiot."

The Crow youth arose from the ground about a hundred yards easterly of the corral. The horses faced in his direction, heads up, ears pointing. They had been as surprised as were the men on the porch.

Gus called, "Come ahead."

The youth kept the horses between himself and the men on the porch until they saw him, then he called again. "I lost my horse."

Gus sank down on the bench. "Come on over here."

As the youth came around the corral toward the porch Hezekiah called to him from the doorway. "What you doin' this far from home?"

Long Walker made no attempt to reply until he was so close he would not have to yell, then he said, "I left the horse in a gully."

"An' forgot to tie him," growled Hezekiah.

The Crow was within porch shade when he replied. "No! I tied him!"

Doug was beginning to have a hunch.

He asked if Long Walker had seen an Indian on a horse atop a knoll. Long Walker had not. He asked to see Johnny.

They took him inside where he stood like a copper statue looking at young Tremaine.

Doug took Gus aside. "That bronco I seen watchin' me. He could have stole the horse, an' if he did, why then it means them bastards is pretty much around us. Got us cut off."

"Why would they steal the horse? They're bein' *coyote*, Doug. If they stole the horse they'd know we'd hear about it an' that we would figure it could be them."

"Maybe they're short of saddle animals. Durin' that fire there was In'ian horses stampedin' every which way."

Hezekiah came over to say, "According to the lad, his people's scouts found sign of many broncos comin' on to the mesa from the east."

The lost horse was forgotten. If a

war party was advancing from the east the log house and its Texans would be directly in its path.

Gus turned to Long Walker. "Your folks know they're comin' from the east?" he asked using his right arm to point eastward.

Long Walker looked puzzled. "They comin' from the north," he replied, and Gus stared. "From the north! Hell, boy, there's nothin' but firebrands and burnin' stumps in that direction." Gus paused to put a disgusted look on Doug and Hezekiah. "In'ian scouts," he said. "A blind pig could do better." He faced Long Walker again. "You go tell your pa they're comin' from the east — directly toward our part of the mesa."

Long Walker did not argue, he simply said, "They got my horse."

Gus's disgust mounted. "Come with me. We'll give you a horse. Where's your weapons?"

Long Walker reacted to the Texan's annoyance. "I don't have none."

Gus said, "For Chris'sake, boy. What's your pa thinkin' of lettin' you ride over here without a weapon!" Gus went to Johnny's bunk, took the shell belt and holstered Colt from its peg, handed them to Long Walker and jerked his head.

As they went in the direction of the corral Doug said, "Hezekiah, if they're short of horses maybe that's why they're comin' in our direction. Sure as hell they been scoutin' up the mesa an' seen our corral."

Hezekiah went to the doorway to watch Gus cut out an animal for the Indian youth. He said, "Son of a bitchin' damned In'ians!"

Gus lingered at the corral watching Long Walker heading due west. It was open country as far as a man could see in that direction. Hezekiah and Doug came to the corral to also watch, carrying their Winchesters.

While watching the young Crow, Gus said, "He told me his pa didn't know he was comin' over here."

7

Dawn after a Long Night?

WHATEVER the Crow reaction to the news Long Walker brought, and it could be assumed tribal scouts would not deviate from their contention that the hostiles were approaching from the north, Black Thunder called a council. Most of those Indians, anxious about an impending reprisal attack, were of the opinion that a strong party of scouts should be sent easterly.

Black Thunder agreed.

For the Texans, with one of them incapacitated, their forted-up advantage would be diminished by one pair of weapons. What Hezekiah wanted to know was exactly where the hostiles were and how many were in the war party, something which Doug dryly said they would certainly find out soon.

Gus got a cud tucked into his cheek, filled a cup with coffee and went to stand near the only window in the log house, which was facing eastward in the front wall and because there was no glass had a stout pair of shutters to keep light in after dark and mosquitos out.

The land as far as he could see was empty. The stillness was deafening. If the hostiles came it might be after sunset, otherwise they would be visible for a mile before they could get close.

Gus spat out the glassless window and thought of something that had happened before he was born, something every Texan learned very early. 5,000 Mexican federal troops had overwhelmed and killed 150 forted-up defenders of a place called the Alamo. It had required thirteen days to do it but Mexican General Santa Anna had never faltered.

Gus, Doug and Hezekiah might be facing a disproportionate number of Indians and, as Gus considered the dying day from the window, he had to believe it would not require thirteen days but the end would be the same.

Hezekiah came over to say Johnny was hot to the touch. Gus turned. "You got any more of that white powder the old man give you?" he asked.

Hezekiah's response was inflectionless. "I lanced the sore, squeezed all the matter out and dosed it with the rest of that powder. Gus, that powder don't seem to do no good."

They went to bedside. Johnny had soaked his clothing with perspiration, it trickled from his upper lip and his forehead. When he opened his eyes it seemed to Gus that when the youth looked at them he was looking through them. There was no flicker of recognition.

He went for a cup of coffee which Doug handed him as they looked steadily at each other. Not a word passed between them because Hezekiah was standing at bedside and each time anyone had said Johnny did not look good, Hezekiah would fiercely contradict them.

Gus returned to the window with his coffee. An old midwife had once told him that if folks had enough perception they could smell approaching death.

Gus was crowding forty, he was younger than Doug or Hezekiah. His life had been a series of what folks called 'adventures' and which he rarely dwelt upon, but now as he stood at the window he recalled other bad situations: none as hopeless as his present condition.

He drained the cup, set it on the table, took his Winchester and was heading toward the door when Doug said, "You go out there'n likely you'll never come back."

Gus passed outside, closed the door and wrinkled his nose like a hunting dog and also blocked in squares of the area for either anything that might resemble a redskin silhouette or movement.

He found neither.

Some men might have felt differently but Gus hadn't had an illusion of safety since he'd been big enough to handle weapons.

He got rid of his cud, sidled soundlessly along the log wall northward and watched their corralled animals. Like a dog, a horse could detect an alien scent long before peril appeared.

The horses were milling a little, seeking stalks of grass, of which there were none in the corral, drinking at the creek and making muted cranky sounds at one another. If there was an Indian in the gloom the horses had not picked up the scent.

Gus went back inside. Hezekiah was arranging a wet cloth on Johnny's forehead, as he looked up Gus leaned his weapon aside and shook his head.

Doug was doing something women could be relied upon to do when frightened and uncertain, he was working at the stove, doing something which occupied his mind and was somehow reassuring.

Hezekiah left the cot for a cup of coffee. Before tasting it he said, "The Crows've had plenty of time to get over here."

Without missing a stir of stew Doug said, "Most In'ians I've heard about don't fight at night. Some kind of belief they got that someone killed at night wanders forever in darkness in the other world."

Hezekiah snorted. "You know better. 'Paches, Comanches, most In'ians where we come from'd rather attack in the dark."

Doug spooned stew into a bowl and handed it to Hezekiah who took the bowl as he said, "He won't eat."

Doug's retort was brief. "It's not for him, it's for you. When's the last time you ate?"

Hezekiah put the bowl on the table, hoisted the whiskey jug to his right shoulder, turned his head and swallowed three times.

Doug rolled his eyes, pointed to the bowl and nodded his head in Gus's direction. Crandal had no inhibitions and he was hungry. As he sat down Hezekiah made a strange throaty sound and crouched over Johnny Tremaine. Doug and Gus paused to watch as the large, bearded man used the wet rag to mop Tremaine's face. When he had done this he let the rag fall to the floor and sat like stone gazing at Johnny.

Gus did not finish the stew and Doug returned to the cooking area to aimlessly use both hands among pans and the small pile of kindling.

Hezekiah eventually arose and without looking at either of the other men, went out on to the porch. Gus approached the bunk. Johnny wasn't sweating, he was looking at the far wall with drying eyes. Doug came over. "He ain't breathin'," he softly said.

Gus returned to the glassless window, he could make out Hezekiah's slumped silhouette on the bench. Full darkness had arrived. Doug moved the candles so that light would not background Gus and later went to the door but Gus shook his head and Doug went for his weapons, sat at the table cleaning and reloading them.

An owl hooted. Both men inside the cabin waited for the answering hoot. There was none. Doug finished with the guns by wiping them with an oily rag. As he rolled and lighted a smoke using one of the candles, Gus turned from the window. Doug was a chewer. Rarely had Gus seen him smoke.

The owl hooted again, from a different direction this time, more southerly.

Gus spoke to Hezekiah through the window. "Better come inside."

Hezekiah could have been deaf. His large slumped torso did not move.

Gus tried again. "Hezekiah, there's tomahawks out there."

This time the large man straightened on the bench, arose ponderously and entered the cabin. Even in poor light it was clear Hezekiah was holding back feelings both Gus and Doug shared, but not with the same intensity.

Hezekiah went to the bunk, pulled a moth-eaten old brown army blanket over Johnny Tremaine covering him from foot to poll and kept his back to Doug and Gus for a long time afterwards.

Not until an owl hooted again did he turn and now it was harder to see his face because Doug had moved a candle away from Johnny's bunk.

"I want the In'ian who shot him!"

Gus nodded. They all did but during the turmoil identifying a particular Indian was impossible. If there was another way to find this particular big belly, neither Gus nor Doug knew what it was.

Something struck the front wall with considerable force. The Texans gazed at one another. Skulking hostiles whose purpose was surprise wouldn't pitch a rock against the cabin unless they expected a forted-up Texan to open the door, and that idea did not occur to the men inside. They hadn't come down in the last rain.

Hezekiah scowled. "I'd give a pretty to know what them scoundrels is up to."

He had barely made that statement when the sound of the corral gate being swung open broke the still silence of the night. Doug moved toward the door, carbine in hand. Gus caught him. "Blow out the candles," he said, and as Doug turned to obey Gus retrieved his leaning Winchester and spoke sharply to Hezekiah, "If we ever build another house, we put in more'n one window hole and one door."

Hezekiah stood like stone as the cabin was plunged into darkness. He heard Gus open the door, saw Doug moving in the same direction and belatedly took his own saddlegun from its wall pegs to follow. What stopped him in mid-stride was a familiar, youthful voice.

Long Walker spoke from the night, invisible but identifiable by his voice. He called to the men on the porch and the larger, bearded man in the doorway.

"Absaroke take your horses. Drive them toward our village."

Gus sat down in overhang darkness. "Where's Black Thunder?"

The youth seemed to appear up out of the ground as he approached the porch. "He go south, Squawman go north."

"Where's the big bellies?"

"Comin' from east like you said. They want to get around behind 'em." Long Walker came on to the porch, looked at big Hezekiah blocking the doorway and said, "I bring more powder."

Hezekiah was silent as he backed clear of the opening so the young Crow could enter.

It was not a long moment of silence before Long Walker threw back his head and wailed an ululating howl. Gus looked straight ahead at the empty corral. Hezekiah lingered in darkness just inside the door. Doug said, "Hostiles can hear that a damned mile."

Long Walker spoke from the darkness inside. "Black Thunder want you to start fight with 'em."

That made sense, if the stalking hostiles were occupied in front, the Crows would have a better chance of coming in behind them. Gus said, "Ain't nothin' in sight to fight," and Long Walker came out on to the porch. "They comin' strung out wide. Big bellies no fight in night. They come for you when light come again."

Long Walker sank to the ground. "Bad blood," he murmured and Hezekiah nodded in silence.

Gus arose to speak, "How far are the big bellies?"

Long Walker did not know. "Maybe not far. Light come soon."

Gus considered the empty corral and the open country beyond it. Indians who wouldn't fight in darkness would miss an excellent opportunity, and in open country could expect to have casualties in any attack against forted-up enemies after sunrise.

He asked if the Crow scouts knew what had happened to the rest of the Gros Ventres after the fire. Long Walker had spoken to several returning scouts so he could relay what he had been told.

"They go back the way they come. Some never come to a council. Maybe they split off, afraid, go somewhere else."

Gus nodded. After the debacle of the fire there would certainly be turmoil. Even if the warriors sought the stampeded horses, other Gros Ventres would react as whites would. Demoralization was not an exclusive Indian characteristic but in this case Gus thought the fire had accomplished disruption, which was fine with him, even though it evidently had not caused widespread chaos among the fighting Indians.

Hezekiah spoke from the gloom, his booming deep voice sounding unrelentingly fierce. "Let 'em come. Numbers won't matter as long as they're in the open an' we're forted up."

Gus and Doug exchanged a glance. Numbers sure as hell would matter.

Doug addressed Hezekiah. "Them Crows runnin' off the horses ain't the best for us. We can't escape now if we got to."

Hezekiah did not respond, he disappeared back inside where the darkness was complete.

Long Walker turned to depart. Gus growled at him. "You stay, boy. Them hostiles had all night to get plumb around us. They catch you an' they'll slit your pouch an' pull your leg through it."

Long Walker stopped moving. He tilted his face a little as though seeking scent.

Doug added to what Gus had said, "You're afoot an' we don't have no horses. Stay, boy, you'll be better off behind the log walls."

Long Walker gazed in the direction of the darkness beyond the open door.

"Running Dog told me he would die. No powder works against bad blood."

Gus had a question. "Did any Crows come in our direction from your village?"

Long Walker shook his head.

Gus nodded. "Good. We wouldn't want to shoot 'em, an' to us one In'ian looks pretty much like another."

Somewhere in the distance a horse whinnied. All eyes turned in that direction. Long Walker said, "Close."

Gus arose. There was a faint but discernible grey wash to the easterly horizon.

They went inside. Doug dropped the bar into its hangers effectively precluding anyone entering from outside.

Hezekiah lighted one candle. Its light was too weak to do more than let them see one another as shadows.

He went to the table with a heavy small box, counted out handgun and saddle-gun ammunition, neatly made three piles and looked up to say, "There's enough." He cocked his head in Long Walker's direction. "Your folks had all night to get around 'em, didn't they? Then I'd guess we won't have to hold 'em off for too long."

Hezekiah went to Johnny's bunk and returned with Tremaine's saddle-gun which he handed the young Crow. He also shoved two handfuls of bullets toward the edge of the table where Long Walker stood. "In my experience In'ians is poor shots. Maybe you'll do better. Check 'n see if Johnny's gun's fully charged."

As Long Walker eased back the slide to expose a brass casing Hezekiah rolled his eyes. "Not that way, boy. See this here thing? You pull it out and feed bullets into the hole where it was. You'll know when it's charged; it won't take no more bullets."

Doug crossed to the cooking area. His intention was to fire up the coffee pot. He did not get it done. With the pale sky turning softly pink they all heard a loping horse. Gus went to the window, stood beside it and peered around the frame.

He barely saw the rider before a blinding muzzle blast made him wince. The slug passed through the window hole and embedded itself in the far wall above dead Johnny's bunk.

Gus closed the window cover.

For what seemed an eternity to the waiting Texans there was not a sound. Long Walker said, "Brave up strongheart," referring to the solitary mounted Indian who had raced past the cabin.

No one commented. Gus regretted not having fired back although his chance of hitting the racing horseman would have been a lot less than good.

He remained by the window and eventually eased the wooden shutter open a crack to peer out. Daylight was strengthening even though as yet there was no sun.

Doug asked if Gus saw anything. Instead of answering Gus shook his head.

Doug turned back to his cooking

area. He was not particularly hungry. None of them would be now, but coffee was always welcome. He fired up a little patch of kindling. The smell permeated the cabin and as coffee heated that aroma also spread.

Outside the sun was coming, so was something else. From his spying place Gus saw Indians. With no cover until they reached the corral they were pushing bushes in front. In some places that ruse would have worked, but not anywhere around the log house because there were no stands of underbrush. Gus shook his head and beckoned to Hezekiah who crossed to the window and also peeked out.

Hezekiah very methodically raised his Winchester, eased it out the crack Gus had made by opening the shutter, and had to crouch far over to snug back the stock and lower his face.

Because there was no way for the detonation to disperse when Hezekiah fired it sounded like a cannon. Gus peeked. Whoever had been behind one big bush was belly-down and fully exposed.

Hezekiah's gunshot brought swift retaliation. Gunfire erupted from all directions, even behind the log house where there was no window and no door.

The attack was fierce and sustained. No one inside dared peek out. Bullets struck the outer logs with a solid sound. If the logs hadn't been green there might have been cracks and splinters. As it was they absorbed each projectile without effort. Nothing short of a cannon could penetrate those walls.

There were shouts and howls amid the gunfire. Hezekiah yelled above the gun thunder that the Indians were keeping up their gunfire so they could get close enough to set the house afire.

Gus shook his head. The logs were no more than six months old. Too green to burn.

Doug did an odd thing, he brought two

tin cups of black coffee and consistent with Doug's bizarre behaviour with gunfire making conversation impossible, Hezekiah and Gus accepted the cups, nodded to Doug and stood at the table sipping.

What diverted Gus was that during a reloading lull he thought he heard someone on the porch near the barred door. He put down the tin cup, sidled toward the door and listened, but the volley-firing started. He considered the window whose slab closure had been riddled and decided whoever was out there could only be seen if he cracked the door a mite. Six-gun in hand he carefully lifted the *tranca*, eased it aside soundlessly, cocked his handgun and grasped the opening handle. Doug and Hezekiah were watching, as still as logs.

He eased the door open a crack at the exact time two bullets struck it wrenching the opening wider.

Gus had a good sighting. Two Indians were blowing tinder into a small fire against the front wall. Gus fired twice, closed the door and remained to one side of it as a furious volley nearly splintered the door.

8

A Sound of Thunder

THE hostiles were as close as the corral, some still used uprooted large plants of underbrush for cover. The gunfire had intermittent lapses for reloading but there was no mistaking the ferocity of the attack nor its objective, which was to overwhelm the Texans.

Behind the house gunfire was sporadic and less powerful than the attack in front and on both sides of the cabin. That the big bellies would try to set fires on the north and south sides where there was no window did not worry the Texans. What did worry them was that their log house, erected as a solid square, an ideal fortress, had no gun ports. Only in front where the window and door had been placed could they return gunfire, and as long as the Indians pressed the attack — and had enough ammunition to sustain it — the defenders could only return the gunfire at great risk.

For the second time, when there was a lull, Gus told Hezekiah their biggest mistake was not to provide gun slots in the walls.

Hezekiah acted as though he had not heard the complaint. His thoughts were on the Crows supposedly closing in from the rear of the Gros Ventres. He told Gus unless this happened soon the big bellies would sure as hell swarm over the defenders.

It did not help that Long Walker began his death chant. The Texans did not have to know Plains Indian customs to understand. The Crow youth had yet to fire Johnny's carbine.

He got his chance by accident. One of the big bushes was sidling toward the south corner of the pole corral which he saw through a large hole in the riddled door. He stopped chanting, worked Johnny's Winchester through the hole, took long aim and fired. The bush fell against corral stringers and whoever had been behind it let out a howl audible over the gun-thunder.

Doug smiled at Long Walker.

The reaction to this was a series of enraged yells and an increase in the firing from the hostiles. Doug spoke loudly to Gus. "He must have winged a war leader."

Hezekiah stood flattened on the south side of the door waiting for one of those lulls. When it came he shoved his barrel through the same hole in the door and fired off six shots as fast as he could lever up and squeeze the trigger. Whether he hit anyone no one ever knew, but he did make several broncos beyond the corral drop flat.

Hezekiah went to the jug for two swallows. He was sweat-soaked. Gus was tempted to use the same door hole but instinct warned him and he moved instead to the shattered shutter, but the attackers knew by now those were the only two places from which the defenders could fire and shot toward them.

Doug found where a piece of chinking between logs had been torn out and leaned to peer out. A tall Indian was approaching from behind the cabin. He passed hesitantly down the north side, his full attention on the attackers in front.

Doug raised his Winchester. The crack was not large enough. He leaned the carbine aside, poked his six-gun through the opening, waited until he could not miss and fired.

The hostile sprang into the air like an antelope and collapsed in a sprawl. For moments some of the attackers in front stopped shooting. They had evidently considered the sides of the cabin safe. Now they knew differently.

Gus borrowed a page from Doug's book and explored the walls for other places where bullets had knocked the chinking out.

Hezekiah too, squinted for openings.

It was Long Walker who discovered a place where chinking had been blown out from between two logs in the front wall for a distance of about eighteen inches. Most of that narrow space was too tight for carbine barrels, but all of it could accommodate handguns.

Black powder weapons made smoke. Even in bright daylight visibility was less than perfect where any number of weapons were being fired that used black powder. Inside the cabin there was less smoke but the smell was strong. Outside the smoke was thicker.

No one knew how many hostiles were attacking but it had to be a sizable war party. Black powder smoke hung in the air like soiled fog.

Long Walker jerked his head and Gus approached him. The youth pushed Johnny's six-gun through the crack, leaned down and fired. He had no target so the shot went wild.

Gus had to lean to see outside, gunsmoke made discernment difficult, but one way to see where a hostile was to watch for an oily mushroom and fire into the centre of it. He and Long Walker emptied their handguns, flattened aside to reload, turned back and again fired their handguns empty.

Hezekiah came over, he had to hunch low to see out. As he straightened back he said, "You put a crimp in 'em."

For a fact the hostile gunfire was slackening. Gus spoke to no one when he said, "They likely damn near shot themselves out."

He was more correct than he knew. The attackers continued to occasionally fire as several withdrew easterly where they had left their horses and their packs.

Hezekiah tanked up at the water bucket, leaned aside his Winchester and sat down at the table, seemingly impervious to the occasional bullet striking logs.

The window shutter had been nearly shot completely away. It sagged on its pair of leather hinges.

The door was in better shape, but

just barely. It was thick slab wood. It had been penetrated at least two dozen times. What prevented it from splintering was the stout draw bar which rested in two hangers, one on each side.

Bullets had only penetrated the front wall where they had shattered mud chinking between logs.

Hezekiah twisted toward his companions and garrulously said, "Where'n hell is them damned Crows?"

No one replied.

Long Walker, watching from the elongated slit, said he was hungry. The Texans stared at him and while they were doing so Long Walker eased his six-gun through between the logs and fired twice.

Someone swore blasphemously in English. Long Walker jerked his gun from the slit and flattened against the wall, just in time. Four gunshots erupted almost simultaneously. Those who had fired could not see the narrow slit but they clearly saw where the gunsmoke mushroomed.

Hezekiah scowled, mopped off sweat and said, "Renegade white man among 'em?"

It was a reasonable surmise but not necessarily an accurate one. Gros Ventres were Hidatsa Sioux, the largest family of tribesmen and the ones who had more contact with whites than other tribesmen. English as a second language was common among them although as a rule they refused to use it, especially among whites.

Someone out behind the log house called loudly in a language none of the defenders understood. He was answered by someone hidden beyond the corral.

After that was a long lull when no shots were exchanged and Hezekiah cursed the Crows who were supposed to be coming behind the big bellies. He ended his tirade with an exclamation.

"This's got to end soon. We're gettin' low on ammunition."

Long Walker approached the large, bearded man and held out one hand with bullets on the palm. Hezekiah looked from the outstretched hand to the youthful face looking up at him and softly smiled. "You keep 'em," he said. "We ain't whipped yet."

The lull with an occasional gunshot ran on. After a long period of this intermittent gunfire Gus tanked up at the water bucket, mopped off sweat and said, "Them ones they sent for their packs had time to return, unless they left their horses one hell of a distance away."

Doug, the inherent optimist, said, "Maybe they run into the Crows."

This notion certainly had its appeal. Unless that had happened, or a miracle occurred, three whites and a young tomahawk were going to die before sunset as sure as day followed night.

There was no way out and no animals to get astride to make a run for it if that had been possible.

What actually happened no one expected. First, there was a distant sound of thunder — which wasn't thunder — then came the reverberation that seemed to come from beneath the ground.

The big bellies stopped firing. When that happened the unnerving sound gradually grew louder. Someone called out from among the hostiles. He got no reply.

Gus swore. The sound seemed to emanate from the west and there was no way to see out in that direction. Attackers and defenders could feel the ground make a kind of drum-roll reverberation.

Long Walker went to the back wall and used his pistol barrel to strike chinking but although bullets could shatter it his best efforts did not dislodge anything.

Doug exclaimed what had just occurred to him. "Gawddamned earthquake!"

Every Texan knew about earthquakes. Possibly the north-country Indians did too, but Gus's scepticism made him say, "If it is I'll never say gawddamn again as long as I live."

The tremor increased; with it there was an increase in that sound of distant thunder.

Gus peeked between the logs. He saw three hostiles standing in plain sight, heads cocked listening, evidently forgetting the attack. One of them pointed to the sky where a solitary streamer of a dark rain cloud seemed not to be moving.

Long Walker spoke softly but audibly when he said, "Great Spirit comes."

Gus couldn't resist a laconic observation about that. "In the nick of time."

Hezekiah stood erect. "Horses!" he exclaimed.

They swept up in a trailing big cloud of dust, hundreds of them running straight toward the cabin, where they split off, half going around it to the south, half going around to the north.

A big belly yelled and emptied his Winchester.

Within moments the horses shattered

the pole corral and charged beyond it. Attackers fired weapons as they fled in all directions. They were easy targets but none of the men inside the log house went to the places where they could fire.

Horses struck the building and caroomed off it. The smell of dust and horse sweat filtered inside. Hezekiah leaned his Winchester aside, removed the *tranca* and opened the door a crack.

Dust as thick as smoke made visibility difficult. All he saw was running horses. He closed the door, replaced the draw bar and stared at Gus. If he'd had something to say it wouldn't have been audible as long as horses rattled the earth, the log walls, and continued to stream around the cabin as though driven by the Devil.

There was an occasional distant gunshot, otherwise Long Walker's 'Great Spirit' had effectively lifted the siege and saved the defenders.

Doug wagged his head like a bull at

fly-time. He was at a loss as were his two companions. Only Long Walker beamed. Gus eyed the youth thinking it must be a wonderful thing to have faith.

Dust hung in the air, the quaking ground seemed to be lessening and somewhere an Indian called out. Long Walker shoved Johnny's six-gun into his waist band and went to the door.

Hezekiah moved to prevent him from opening it but not quickly enough.

Long Walker cracked the door and sang out.

Through the dust an ancient wraith appeared, shrivelled as a prune. He had an Indian's single horsehair rein in his left hand, an ancient musket in the other hand. His mount was wild eyed with distended nostrils. Its sides heaved like bellows, sweat dripped as the horse bobbed his head and blew its nose.

Hezekiah went to stand in the doorway behind Long Walker. He spoke to Gus and Doug without facing around. "Running Dog," he said. "I'll be a son of a bitch!"

The old medicine man slid to the ground, held out the single rein toward Long Walker and came up on to the porch. Long Walker held the excited horse as he spoke to the old man. Running Dog answered in a sort of harangue.

Long Walker interpreted, his tone of voice clearly reflecting astonishment. "Him an' old women drive Crow horses. They heard guns."

Hezekiah gazed at the old shaman. He asked Long Walker how old Running Dog was. The answer supplied a fair estimate. "He was old at Little Big Horn where Yellow Hair got killed."

Hezekiah inclined his head slightly. Custer's fiasco had been about twenty-five years earlier. Hezekiah held out his hand. The old man did not take the hand, he reached above it and briefly gripped Hezekiah's forearm.

Three mounted Crow women came

around the cabin, reined to an impassive halt and looked at bigbearded Hezekiah. One raised a hand to her mouth to stifle a snicker. The other, older women sat like stone, expressionless and dusted over with what could not be avoided driving large numbers of horses — sweaty dust.

Two other women came around from the south side of the house. They were younger. One spoke shyly to Long Walker. His answer poured out with words running into each other.

Gus shouldered past to the porch. Doug also came outside. Running Dog raised rheumy old dark eyes with muddy whites. He stared straight at Hezekiah. In some way the old man's thought passed to Hezekiah, who gravely inclined his head.

Running Dog also nodded as he said something for Long Walker to interpret. "Bad blood."

The dust lingered although the horses were far easterly, slackening their gait somewhat. Several halted then turned back. Gus recognised them but there was a lot of patching to be done before the corral would hold them.

The old man brushed past, entered the cabin, went beside the bunk with the old army blanket covering dead Johnny Tremaine, made motions with his arms and hands, leaned low to do a surprising thing. He made the sign of the Cross on Johnny's shroud.

From a considerable distance there was a burst of ragged gunfire. Gus made a guess the big bellies had run into Black Thunder and Squawman's contingent of Crows.

Several of the mounted women watered their horses at the creek, then dropped down to also drink. As they arose one woman faced Hezekiah and jutted her jaw. "Long Walker my boy," she said, which was just about the extent of her knowledge of English. Hezekiah told her except for her son the big bellies would have caught him and his companions flat-footed.

The woman smiled without understanding what Hezekiah had said, but his tone of voice had told her all she had to know.

Besides Running Dog there were three other old men. The women, normally prohibited by custom from taking part in men's work, were both young and old. There were six of them.

Doug sank down on the bench. During the fight he had felt alert and willing but now, with dust settling, the running horses no longer in sight and less noise, he slumped.

Long Walker sat down beside him, seemingly neither tired nor anxious. He said, "Great Spirit send horses."

Doug nodded. It didn't matter who or what had sent them. What mattered to Doug Hardy was that he was alive, which he had just about abandoned hope of being most of this day.

Hezekiah got the jug. Running Dog waved it away. The women remained with their horses at the creek. They had done themselves proud. They had also gone against tribal custom. They reverted now to their traditional status. They would not approach where the men on the porch talked.

Hezekiah used Long Walker to interpret as he told Running Dog he had been certain he and his Texans could not have lasted much longer.

The wizened old man regarded Hezekiah with an expression of hard humour and spoke. Long Walker put it into English.

"Old white man with whiskers tough as boiled owl. He would have made it."

Hezekiah smiled at Running Dog who smiled back, then watched as the jug was passed among the Texans and told Long Walker in the language of the Absaroke that white men get made strong because of bad water they drank.

9

A Night to Remember

IT was close to sundown when a few straggling Crow men of war appeared. They were astride bone-weary animals and did not push them.

Black Thunder was not among them but Squawman was, riding a speckled roan at least sixteen hands tall.

Other tribesmen were farther back scuffing up dust as they drove the retrieved Crow horses and other animals without cropped ears, evidently caught as the big bellies fled. Not all had been able to get ahorseback.

Several drovers waved or held aloft their weapons. Squawman dismounted at the wrecked corral, found an upright to tether his horse to and approached the porch where Hezekiah and Gus waited.

The tall Indian acted tired. Gus went after some water which Squawman drank, then said, "We got 'em from behind."

Hezekiah nodded. "How many?"

Squawman leaned on an upright which supported the overhang.

"We killed eleven. Maybe thirty, maybe forty. Didn't have no scouts behind. We come on to 'em — big surprise."

Gus eyed the tall man. "Any captives?"

Squawman looked steadily at Gus. "No captives," then he changed the subject. "It got crazy when the horses run into 'em. They run back toward us. It was like shootin' ducks on a pond."

Hezekiah mentioned Running Dog and the tall Crow looked past at the open door when he said, "He done bad. He brought other old men and the women. They got no place in a fight."

A handsome woman came slowly from the creek. She heard what

164

Squawman had said. She didn't have to know much English to understand. She stopped beyond the porch and addressed the tall Crow in their language. He did not even turn to face her, not even after she had spoken. He simply said, "Make men look bad when squaws interfere."

Hezekiah bristled. "Look bad? What'n hell are you talkin' about? If we'd waited for you'n Black Thunder to show up we'd've got massacreed."

The handsome woman moved into failing shade. Dusk was coming. She smiled slightly at Hezekiah. "Long Walker said we done proud."

Gus cleared his throat. This was one of those discussions that led nowhere. If the warriors did not like what their women had done that was their affair. As far as the Texans were concerned the women under Running Dog had saved their lives. He arose, went after the jug, returned with it and handed it around. Squawman swallowed once and coughed. When the whiskey took hold he finally faced the woman. His tone was softer than it had been. She nodded and returned to the creek where the other women were.

He watched her go then faced Hezekiah again. Doug sat slouched and also watched the woman leave. He made a droll remark. "Among us whites we show thanks for women who help. It don't cost anythin' to say thanks." He arose and went inside.

Dusk settled, the women, Running Dog, the other old men with him, got astride and left.

Hezekiah watched the handsome woman. Riding stirrup with her was Long Walker. He was talking a mile a minute.

Doug had the candles lighted and was fussing at the cooking area. He wasn't hungry, he was bone tired, but he heated the stew for the others.

Hezekiah ate as did Gus, but out of habit. Afterwards Hezekiah hefted the whiskey jug. It was less than a third full.

The following morning they set about rebuilding the corral. In the afternoon they scouted for the cattle. The racket caused by the battle of the previous day had sent them in every direction.

They found most of the cows and two bulls before dark. They also found several dead big bellies whom they dragged out a ways and piled rocks atop them until it got too dark to find boulders.

Doug spoke aside to Gus while Hezekiah was washing at the creek. "We got to bury him. He's beginnin' to smell."

The next morning Gus carried Johnny in his old army blanket where the creek flooded in spring and the ground was soft, and went back for digging tools. Hezekiah said nothing but he worked with Gus and Doug squaring up the sides of an earthen grave over three feet deep. He helped lower the body, then leaned on a shovel unable to help fill the grave. Before the work was finished he left and did not reappear until Doug and Gus had topped off the mound and had got astride to look for more cattle, then Hezekiah went alone to the grave site, knelt and read from a dogeared little Bible he'd carried for thirty years. Afterwards he pocketed the Bible and sat down Indian fashion, legs folded, and did something else Indians did, he rocked back and forth. He'd had plans for Johnny. He'd had other plans as well and usually they either ended badly or did not culminate in anything other than disappointment.

He did not return to the cabin until after dark when Doug and Gus were in their soogans.

The following day the three of them completely rebuilt the corral with very little conversation. Hezekiah was withdrawn, almost grim.

In the afternoon Black Thunder arrived wearing his war shirt and leading several horses by the simple expedient of leading one with a rope, the other horses' headstalls were braided into the tail of the horse ahead.

He nodded approval of the rebuilt corral, put the horses in, closed the gate and faced around as Hezekiah came from the cabin. For the spokesman English came hard. He said, "You done good. Many dead big bellies." He held out his right hand with the fist closed. When Hezekiah held out his hand the spokesman dropped a heavy doeskin pouch in it. "White man's yellow dirt."

Hezekiah knew what the pouch contained. He also knew that as a rule Indians living apart from whites did not share white enthusiasm about gold.

He said, "You keep it. We done what we had to because there wasn't nothin' else we could do."

Black Thunder did not hold out his hand. He scowled. Among Indians no one refused a present. The spokesman changed the subject of their conversation.

"You bury boy?"

Hezekiah nodded without speaking.

Black Thunder fished in his parfleche, brought forth something folded into a scrap of old gingham and handed it to Hezekiah. "Running Dog believe in Messican Gawd. He sent you this to bury in the grave."

Hezekiah unwrapped the small packet. Inside was a very old Mexican crucifix of solid gold embedded with red stones.

Black Thunder said, "Running Dog says your God will know now to take care of boy." Black Thunder jutted his jaw at Hezekiah's hand. "Your God keep them who have that metal."

Black Thunder changed the subject again. "Squawman come with more horses. He come with Long Walker." The old man eyed Hezekiah unblinkingly then turned to go to his tethered horse, get astride and ride northward a short distance before turning westerly.

Hezekiah went inside, placed the crucifix on the table beside the whiskey jug, did not explain anything and tossed the pouch of gold down.

Doug considered the pouch, the crucifix, and again the pouch. "Gold?" he asked.

Hezekiah nodded without speaking. Johnny's empty bunk held his attention briefly before he put his back to it. Gus hefted the pouch while Doug busied himself at his cooking area.

That evening they ate like horses, and during the meal someone out in the night opened the corral gate, which they heard, sprang up reaching for their weapons.

When they were outside the gate had been closed. There were several strange animals in among their own stock.

Long Walker spoke from the corral. "Take place of ones you see no more."

Lanky Squawman put it better. "Hidatsa horses we capture. You had nine, now you got nine again."

Hezekiah leaned his Winchester aside as did Doug and Gus. They went out to the corral and Gus, who was more horseman than cowman, grunted his approval. The Hidatsa horses were tucked up, otherwise as nearly as he could see in the darkness all they needed to be worthwhile was feed and lots of it.

Squawman got astride his tall horse. Long Walker also got mounted but he seemed less willing to leave. He said, "We good as soldiers."

Hezekiah grinned which none of the others could see. "Better," he told the young Crow.

"Where you put Johnny?"

Hezekiah did not answer, he raised a thick arm, pointed and went inside. Squawman said something and Long Walker followed the tall man into the night riding westerly. Doug thought it would be close to sun-up before they got back to their rancheria.

In the morning they rode three horses and herded the others out to graze. Hezekiah and Gus went cattle hunting. They left Doug with the horses because the Hidatsa horses might wander. They didn't; they were content to graze in tall grass with the other horses.

When the horses were full Doug drove them back to the corral where they scuffled among themselves at the creek.

Doug hauled his saddle, blanket and bridle to the porch and dumped them in thickening shade. He was straightening around to go inside when a sound of roiled air made him swing back around.

The Indian had his fleshing knife held low as he sprang. Doug had a second to turn sideways, even so the blade sliced through his vest and shirt.

Doug grabbed for his holstered Colt. The Indian came around with the agility of a cougar. He rushed Doug again, this time head-on.

Doug could not draw his gun in time. The Indian struck him hard with a lowered shoulder. Again the knife flashed. This time Doug kicked as hard and as fast as he could. The Indian grunted but did not waver.

With his back to the log wall Doug groped for the holster again but the Indian was too close as he lunged with the knife.

Doug struggled to move sideways. He succeeded but the knife followed. Doug felt something like a bee sting and felt the wetness.

He locked both arms around the Indian, strained as hard as he could, lifted the Indian off his feet, whirled and slammed him against the logs.

This time his attacker slumped. Doug stepped back, shot his right fist from the shoulder with all his weight behind it. The Indian's head struck logs for the second time. This teeth-rattling strike was followed up with two more, a left and a right fist, one to the face of the Indian, the other to sink wrist-deep in his soft parts.

The fight was over. The Indian slid down the wall and fell sideways. Doug picked up the knife and flung it away. He leaned to grope for other weapons, felt giddy and went to the bench where his legs turned slack.

The knife slash had caught him across the middle. It was bleeding but there was no sense of pain, just weakness. Doug arose, grabbed the Indian by the hair, dragged him inside and lighted candles.

He had to sit down again. In better light he removed both his vest and shirt to examine the gash.

It wasn't deep but it bled, soaking Doug's britches and spattering the floor.

He got a blanket, tore it into strips and bound his middle tightly. Blood seeped through but the bleeding seemed to have been inhibited by the pressure.

Hezekiah and Gus returned with the sun reddening as it sank westerly. As they were off-saddling at the corral Gus stumbled over something. It was a large fleshing knife. Hezekiah looked at it, at the cabin and crossed the intervening distance rapidly.

He and Gus first saw the inert Indian, then they saw blood and Doug's glazed glance.

Gus washed the wound from the drinking bucket. Hezekiah examined it by holding a candle close and straightened up to say, "Three more inches, Doug, an' you'd have been carrying your guts in a bucket."

They worked over Hardy for a solid hour. Staunched most of the bleeding with clean, tight bandaging, got whiskey down Doug and asked what had happened. He told them speaking in a tired voice.

They got him to his bunk, settled him and went to the Indian, who had not moved since he'd been dragged inside. Gus knelt, flopped the Indian on his back, held a candle close and looked at Hezekiah. "He's dead."

Hezekiah nodded his head. "Good thing he ain't a Crow, his hair's long. Big belly . . . ?"

Gus arose looking at the Indian. "I'll fetch Running Dog. Don't get in front of the light, there could be more of 'em out there."

Hezekiah stood in the doorway with his Winchester until Gus was mounted and on his way. When he returned inside, he barred the door and asked Doug a question which the wounded man did not answer. He was sound asleep.

Hezekiah took a candle to examine the Indian. When he would have raised him the Indian's head fell far backward. Hezekiah eased him down, gently worked his head from side to side and grunted. The Indian's neck was broken.

There was an old saying that rattlesnakes travel in pairs. Maybe they did, Hezekiah did not know, what he did know was that while stronghearts often attacked alone there was no guarantee this one had been alone.

He doused all the candles except the one near Doug's bed, made sure his Winchester was fully loaded and stood in darkness near the splintered window, listening. There was not a sound. There wouldn't be, not if other skulkers were out there in the night. If Doug hadn't been helpless Hezekiah would have gone outside in the night. He was an individual without fears and more to the point on this night, he was experienced.

Whether the dead bronco's friends would attack in darkness or not, if Hezekiah found one, that would not apply to him. He had fought many times in the night. As a seasoned Confederate survivor he knew ways to use darkness other men did not.

He paced the cabin, pulled on the jug a couple of times, went to stand over Doug like a bear, and finally went to the door.

If there were other hostiles out there it might be better to let them do the hunting. He sighed and went to sit at the table. It was a long night. Twice he responded to Doug's groans. The last time he spooned whiskey down Hardy. After that the injured Texan seemed to sink into a very deep sleep.

Without realizing it Hezekiah fell asleep at the table. What roused him was the sound of horses at the corral. He picked up the Winchester sure hostiles were out there to run off their animals. The sun hadn't risen but dawn-light was spreading.

He saw Gus and the old Crow. He did not see a third person until they turned toward the cabin. He met them at the door, and stopped dead still. The third person was a woman. The one who had said Long Walker was her boy, the squaw who challenged Squawman near the porch the day they had chased the horses to scatter the big bellies.

Gus brushed past followed by the wizened old medicine man. The woman hesitated, looked straight at Hezekiah then also came inside.

Running Dog used three candles. He did not unwrap the bandaging but spoke aside to the woman, who said, "He wants to know how deep?"

Hezekiah held up a finger. "Like maybe the tip of my finger, but he bled like a stuck hawg."

The woman spoke to Running Dog who produced one of those little doeskin pouches, handed it to Hezekiah and again spoke to the woman. She asked how wide the gash was and when Hezekiah gestured the old man wagged his head and spoke again. This time Long Walker's mother hesitated to interpret. Gus got a bench for her from the table but Hezekiah neither moved nor spoke. He stared steadily at the woman awaiting her interpretation.

She finally said, "He wants to take away cloth."

Her hesitancy was justified, Hezekiah scowled and shook his head.

The old man considered Hezekiah for a moment before speaking again. This time the woman interpreted without hesitation. "He say big cut like that never come together by itself."

She sat on the bench Gus had provided regarding the large, bearded man. Running Dog got a bench, dragged it to bedside and also sat down.

Gus asked the woman if Running Dog had ever doctored a knife slash before. She smiled slightly and nodded her head. "Many times."

Hezekiah still scowled. "The bleedin's near stopped. Take off that bandage an' it'll start again. He's lost a sight of blood."

The wizened old Crow sat in silence regarding Doug. He eventually spoke quietly and the woman interpreted again. "He say unless cut fixed this one could get bad blood too."

Hezekiah busied himself cheeking a cud of molasses-cured. When that was settled he looked at Gus, who shrugged his shoulders as he spoke. "He was right about Johnny. I think he's right, that's too wide a cut to heal by itself."

Hezekiah asked the woman if Running Dog had gut to sew the wound with. She shook her head. Hezekiah again faced Gus. "That powder won't work.

It didn't save Johnny."

The woman spoke quickly. "It no work if the blood has got bad. With this one it might work. The wrapping looks clean."

Gus was regarding the sleeping man when he said, "It's like before, Hezekiah. You'n me don't know what to do. The old man might, which is more'n we can say."

Hezekiah tapped Running Dog on the shoulder. When the old man looked up Hezekiah solemnly nodded his head.

Running Dog left the cabin and returned with his old army saddle pouch. He put a candle on the table, told the woman to soak the bandage until it could be removed without sticking and gazed at Hezekiah. This time the woman arose as she interpreted. "He say if you got turtle rattle you go outside and shake it an' make prayer."

Hezekiah had no turtle rattle, no rattle of any kind, but he did go outside. Whether he prayed out there or not he never said. He hadn't wanted to watch what would take place inside. He had a feeling of having been through this before.

10

Bloody Hands!

GUS bunched the candles. The old man nodded approval as he groped in the old army bag. The woman soaked the bandage and Doug awakened to stare. Gus said, "The old man's goin' to fix you up."

Doug regarded the wizened, solemn old man, shifted his gaze to the woman and asked who she was.

Her name was Dawn Child, her father was Black Thunder. Her man had died of pox five years before. She didn't say why her man had died because she didn't know, but years later what had happened would be known. During a fierce winter the Mandan people who had for centuries been the inhabitants of the huge plateau, had gone to the soldiers for help. They had been given old army blankets from the army's infirmary where soldiers had been ill with smallpox. In the spring a visitor happened upon a Mandan rancheria of many tipis. There were seven Mandans alive, the others had all died of smallpox for which they had no immunity.

The Mandans never recovered. In fact except for inter-marriage the tribe became extinct. Dawn Child's man had been one of the last Mandans.

Doug returned his attention to the old man who was gingerly working the soaked bandage loose. The process was not particularly painful but Doug occasionally winced and immediately the old man trickled on more water, then went back to work.

There was bleeding. There was also swelling which had been held to a minimum by the tight cloth. Gus leaned as the old Crow used some of the removed bandaging to wipe blood away as he bent to make a narrow-eyed examination. He sprinkled some of his white powder on the injury. There was discolouration, but except for the swelling the wound seemed in process of healing.

The old man carefully put aside something from his bag which had been carefully wrapped in doeskin. He did not look up when he spoke to Dawn Child. He told her to tell Doug what he was going to do was painful and that he must not move.

Doug rolled his eyes and Gus got the jug. Doug swallowed three times. The old man watched him in silence. He knew about bad water. Few Indians his age did not know about whiskey.

He unfolded the small doeskin bundle and Gus stared. It had held a number of the bent spines from what folks called thornpin. The old man bent low, muttered something which the woman interpreted as the old man went to work.

"If you move it will have to be done again. No move, no speak." She nodded at Gus and toward the jug. Doug swallowed three more times. Sweat appeared on his upper lip. He fixed his gaze on the ceiling.

Running Dog only used his thornpins where the opening was widest, which was about half the injury. Each time he hooked one through flesh Gus's fists knotted until the knuckles were white.

Running Dog was methodical. He made each closure after careful consideration. Gus saw sweat dripping from Doug's face and would have offered the jug again but the old man brushed it curtly away. Doug required no more whiskey and the old man was nearly finished.

Dawn Child got a wet cloth to sponge off Doug's face. His fixed gaze on the ceiling ignored her.

Hezekiah came back inside but only passingly watched what was being done, went to the table, sat down and stonily regarded knotted hands.

He knew in his heart Doug Hardy would die. Outside in the hushed night he had felt discouraged. He and Gus would not be able to do what had to be done, there possibly were men in that town down yonder who would hire out, but Hezekiah's supply of hard money was nearly exhausted. Besides, when outsiders heard what had happened on Mandan Mesa it would take more than money to make them come to the plateau.

He was jarred from his reverie when Doug groaned. He glanced over where candlelight brightened the cabin but did not arise.

Dawn Child came to resoak the wet rag. On her way back to the bunk and the light she paused to tell Hezekiah the old man had said he didn't believe Doug had bad blood. Not yet anyway. She smiled at Hezekiah. "He not move. No move until another full moon."

Running Dog was rebandaging the wound when Doug passed out. Gus leaned quickly to listen for breathing. The old man spoke to Dawn Child. She addressed Gus. "Good. Much hurt. When he come out of it, he not move.

Not for many days."

Gus watched Hezekiah go to his soogan and rummage. As he approached Running Dog he held out the small soft pouch Black Thunder had given him. The old man arose unsteadily, ignored the outstretched hand and growled something which made Dawn Child arise. She shook her head at Hezekiah and followed the old man out into the night.

Doug did not awaken until dawn. He moved slightly, ground his teeth and stopped moving. Gus told him what the medicine man had said. Doug stared at them both and closed his eyes.

Gus went out into the new day to herd the horses to graze. During his absence Hezekiah sat beside Doug's bunk in silence.

It was a long time before Doug's eyes opened again and he said, "How much damned whiskey did you pour down me?"

Hezekiah's expression brightened when

189

he replied. If Doug had a whiskey-headache it had to mean what else had been done to him was less painful. He told Hardy what the old man had said about not moving for a month, and Doug frowned. "For a damned month?"

"Unless you want to pull them thornpins loose, for a damned month," Hezekiah replied, and smiled a little. "That's the first tomahawk I ever seen who knew what to do." He arose. "Care for a jolt?"

Doug accepted what Hezekiah poured for him and within half an hour complained about his sore middle and said nothing about the headache.

Before Gus returned in mid-afternoon Hezekiah had got some hot stew down the wounded man. When Gus walked in Doug said, "I got to lie like this for a damned month! How do I pee?"

Gus grinned. "In the stew pan. We'll scour it at the creek."

As days passed Doug's discomfort gradually diminished. Each time he moved it came back with a vengeance. He fretted to whichever of his companions remained with him while the other one rode out.

He had been flat out ten days when Long Walker and his mother came visiting. The youth had trophies for Doug, two ears and an ancient, scarred, single-shot cap and ball pistol. Someone had attempted to embellish the stock with a very poor carving of a buffalo. "Big belly," he told Doug as he placed the trophies on the bunk.

Dawn Child examined the wound with gentle hands. While she was doing this she said Running Dog was her grandfather, his son was Black Thunder.

The Texans were beginning to associate particular Crows with the others. Remembering something, Hezekiah told Dawn Child Black Thunder had told him Long Walker was his boy.

She responded with a small smile. "Long Walker my son. Black Thunder is his grandfather. He always say Long

Walker is his boy."

She left in mid-afternoon. It was a long ride back and Black Thunder had warned her that, after the strongheart's attack upon the white man there could very likely be other hostiles in the area.

After she and Long Walker left Hezekiah went to the porch to wave, and to sit on the bench. He was brooding out there when Gus came out to say Doug was out of his head and seemed to be running a fever.

Hezekiah half arose, sank back down and clasping both hands between his knees nodded his head.

Gus understood, sat down and said, "What I seen of the wound it looks as healthy as a man might expect, with them thornpins in it."

Hezekiah nodded again and still leaned, his hands clasped.

Dusk arrived, day-long heat diminished. Gus made a meal of sorts of which he ate little and Hezekiah did not eat at all. Doug was sleeping, he missed the meal, which was probably just as well.

Days passed, routines established when they had first arrived on the huge mesa were adhered to, except that now there were two men to do the work instead of four.

Hezekiah brought in a bloody bull which he said had been attacked by a cougar. They kept the bull close, washed his wounds then left Doug alone while they went lion-hunting.

When they tracked the cougar by blood spots Hezekiah was grimly pleased. "One thing about longhorns," he told Gus, who already knew the rest of it, "roil one up an' he'll fight a buzz saw."

They treed the big cat far enough north to catch a faint scent of burnt timber. Hezekiah dismounted to take solid aim upwards when Gus brushed his arm and placed a finger over his lips.

The sound was indistinct but

identifiable. Riders were approaching from the east.

They hid their animals, took shelter in some rocks and waited. The first rider was on a gaunt, leggy horse with an army neck brand. The Indians following him all had bloody hands painted on the shoulders of their mounts. When warriors painted the bloody hand symbol on their mounts it signified a suicide war trail, they did not expect to return.

The Indians passed about a hundred yards south of the Texans, riding westerly. Gus said, "The Crow camp sure as hell."

Hezekiah counted the warriors. There were four of them, some with faces painted black, some with zigzag red streaks on their torsos indicating spilt blood. All were armed with Winchesters, pistols, tammiaxes and fleshing knives.

Gus prayed hard their horses would not catch a scent and look northward. Hezekiah prayed differently; he did not want their hidden horses to see or smell the Indian horses and whinny.

It was early afternoon. After the war party had passed Gus said, "They're after scalps an' horses sure as hell."

Hezekiah frowned. "They ain't supposed to fight at night."

Gus's reply was dry. "They got the rest of the day an' all night to scout up the Crow horse herd, hit it like lightning at first light and ride back like hell."

When they returned for the treed cougar it was gone. There was blood on the ground where it had landed. Gus shrugged, as far as he was concerned the big cat no longer mattered. If the cougar had been gored he would eventually die, they had their bull back and while he had been mauled he would recover.

Hezekiah said, "We'd never reach the rancheria in time to warn 'em."

That was too obvious to warrant comment. Gus slouched along with private thoughts. When they were in sight of the cabin he roused sufficiently to say, "Good thing they passed the cabin. That's something to be thankful for."

Hezekiah dismounted at the corral, turned his mount in and waited until Gus was ready then they both went to the cabin, and got a shock.

Doug had somehow got one of the canteens and was drinking from it. As they entered he snarled at them. "A man could die in here for all you two care!"

Doug, a normally tolerant man, showed enough indignation to suggest to his friends that he just might make it after all.

They told him what they had seen. He put the canteen aside as he spoke. "Crows'll have scouts out."

Hezekiah scratched his beard. The Crows would of course have scouts out, but the kind of hostiles he had seen were aware of this. Their kind were sly as wolves. They would know what to expect and how to avoid it.

Doug asked for the jug and Gus

handed it to him. Doug shook it. "One of these days someone's goin' to have to ride down to that town an' get it refilled," he said, swallowed twice, blew out a flammable breath and handed the jug to Gus, who also hoisted it. Hezekiah, the last to shoulder the jug, afterwards put it aside and said, "If it's them big bellies, an' if they stampede Crow horses back easterly, we might fix up a surprise for 'em."

Doug was breathing deeply, the lower the jug's contents got the stronger the corn squeezings got. His eyes sparkled. "Bushwhack 'em. How many was there?"

"Four bloody hands."

Doug smiled, his first smile in weeks. "We can pick 'em off like ducks on a pond."

Gus said, "We? You stay right where you are."

Doug's gaze flashed fire. "You don't leave me in here again with bloody hands around."

Hezekiah sighed and rolled his eyes.

197

He spoke very plainly, the way an adult would address a child. "Doug, you heard what Running Dog said. You bust them thornpins loose an' you'll be months flat out."

Doug snorted. His returning health plus the whiskey made him invincible. "When you go, I go too."

Hezekiah looked helplessly at Gus, who spoke patiently. "Partner, if I got to I'll tie you to that bed. Hezekiah an' me'll do fine."

Doug settled back, closed his eyes and sprang them wide open. "They know we're here. They'll attack the cabin sure as hell."

Hezekiah shook his head. "Not with all they can do runnin' off stole horses. They bypassed the cabin on their way west. We ain't as important to them as horses and whatever hair they can lift. On the way back, maybe they'll come by the cabin." Hezekiah made a wolfish smile.

Doug scowled. "You 'n Gus figure to ambush 'em from the yard?"

"If they come that close," Hezekiah replied and stood up. The little benches they had made were adequate for eating when a man could lean on the table. Otherwise if a man didn't have a backache when he sat down with nothing to lean on, he sure-Lord would have one if he sat long enough.

Gus and Hezekiah went out to look at the injured bull. He wasn't in sight. They went to the corral and leaned there to talk.

Hezekiah was of the opinion that the injured bull had more important things on his mind than worrying about injuries.

Gus let that pass. "We got enough time. After it's plumb dark I'll scout westerly. When I hear 'em comin' I'll come back 'n we can set up the bushwhack. What bothers me is if the Crows is chasin' after the horse thieves. In the dark one tomahawk'll look like another."

Hezekiah nodded. "If it was daylight we could see the bloody hands on their animals. You're right. I expect we got to depend on the Good Lord not to salivate the wrong broncos." Hezekiah paused to pouch a cud and expectorate once before adding a little more. "Two things, Gus. If they go far enough north we'll be hard put to bushwhack 'em, an' if they got friends waitin' somewhere, they'll hear gunshots an' most likely come a-runnin'."

Gus was leaning on a corral stringer gazing at the horses. His final remark was borrowed straight from Hezekiah. "Damned In'ians, nothin' but trouble four ways from the middle."

The big man chuckled and led the way back to the cabin.

Doug was trying to sing *Oh Susanna*. When he couldn't remember the words he hummed.

Hezekiah went to the stew pot. For the first time since his earlier ride with Gus he felt hungry.

Doug had a question that Gus answered shortly. He said, "How d'you know they'll come back this way?"

"Because that's the way they come from, an' if they make off with the horses — drivin' horses in a dead run means the critters won't bunch up, they'll scatter over a wide swath."

Gus went to his bunk and slept fully attired. He did not even remove his shellbelt and holstered Colt. Hezekiah visited with Doug until Hardy dropped off, then Hezekiah went outdoors.

There was a scimitar moon, the corralled animals were sleeping hip-shot except a couple with sore shoulders who were lying down with legs folded under them like dogs.

There was not a sound, the day-long warmth had yielded to darkness. Hezekiah went out as far as Johnny Tremaine's grave and sat on the ground. When he was ready to return to the house it was late. His companions inside were dead to the world. Hezekiah should have been and for a fact he was tired, but not sleepy.

His thoughts drifted backwards and forwards. He thought about Indians, wondered how long it would be before the army rooted out holdouts like Black Thunder's people and drove them on to reservations, and grimaced. When that occurred he and his Texans were going to have more scars than they had now.

He thought about that wizened old man who had been among Mexicans so long. He wondered about Black Thunder and believed he would die fighting before he would be reservationed. Finally, he thought about Long Walker, Johnny Tremaine's friend, was still thinking of him when Gus appeared in the doorway, halted to yawn mightily, then went to the bench, sat down and vigorously scratched inside his shirt as he said, "If we figured this wrong an' them hostiles drive the horses south, we're goin' to be about as useless as tits on a boar."

Hezekiah's mood was resigned and mellow. He spoke on another subject. "If we stay on this mesa sure as hell we're goin' to be involved with In'ians.

One kind or another, an' right now In'ians is trouble any way you look at it." Hezekiah paused to push his legs out and lean back. "Gus, my wanderin' days is over. Like you told me once, no matter where we go we ain't goin' to find a better place to build up a herd. In'ians or no In'ians, we'd ought to settle here. What d'you think?"

Gus yawned again before speaking. "If it ain't In'ians it'll be something else, five foot snowdrifts, bears 'n cougars, rustlers. My pa told me once that there ain't no promises in life. A wise man settles where he needs to an' the rest of it'll take care of itself. But Hezekiah, I'll tell you one thing: if either you or me get put off our feed, one man can't do all that's got to be done up here."

Hezekiah leaned to expectorate then leaned back. "What you're sayin' is that it's a gamble just gettin' out of a man's blankets in the mornin'. Well; you like this place, Gus?"

"I like it fine. For us it's the best

place we been so far."

Hezekiah slowly straightened on the bench, the night had turned chilly. He sat erect with his head cocked. Gus spoke calmly at his side. "Horses, hell of a bunch of them."

They went inside, got their weapons as quietly as they could and a voice reached them from the darkness. "You want to know what I think?" Doug asked, and allowed no time for a reply. "I think this mesa's got some kind of spell on it. In'ians in this country don't fight at night but all the trouble we seen has been mostly at night, an' now I can feel rumblin' in the ground. I'd take it kindly if you'd set my Winchester close to hand in case some braved-up damned strongheart takes a notion to sneak inside."

They put the weapon at his side. As Gus was turning away he offered an admonition. "If you use that thing don't snug it to your shoulder an' don't set up."

Doug's reply was as dry as autumn

leaves. "You mind the outside an' I'll mind the inside."

They returned to the porch, stood silently listening to the identical sound they had heard before in this place. Dozens of running horses. The difference was that the first time the squaws and old men had not raised the yell. This time over the drumroll of frightened horses there were triumphant howls and barking yelps.

Hezekiah went to the north edge of the porch. "They're goin' to go past no more'n a short distance. That don't make much sense."

Gus disagreed. "It makes sense. They can't steer them horses in darkness any more'n you an' me could. Come along."

They left the porch at a trot. The only shelter, and it hadn't helped the last time, was the rebuilt pole corral whose animals were in an agitated state; they milled and snorted, heads held high, ears forward.

Gus led around to the far side of the

corral. The sound was now loud. There was an occasional shout, a yell, and less frequently the whistles of former wild horses reverting to their frightened instincts.

The corralled animals became agitated, they ran, whirled back, kicked at one another and bumped each other. The rebuilt corral was logged to a height of almost six feet and the stringers were green, not brittle as the old corral had been. They could absorb an eight-hundred pound jolt without breaking.

Hezekiah rested his saddle-gun atop the uppermost stringer.

Gus moved to the north-east corner of the corral, waited until he could actually make out running animals before taking a rest with his Winchester. There was dust, invisible but pungently present.

11

The Last Fight

BECAUSE the panicked animals spread wide in their rush two riders veered southward in the direction of the cabin to turn them back. One Indian was waving a blanket and riding a light sorrel horse.

Gus could make out the horse, waited for the Indian to yell as he waved his blanket and the horses were turning back northward, then Gus fired.

The rider went off over the rump of his frightened sorrel, landed hard and as Gus levered up to fire at the second horsethief the man who had been shot off his horse got onto all fours and emptied his six-gun in the direction from which had come the muzzleblast that had knocked him off the horse.

Hezekiah aimed at the flashes. When he fired the Indian half arose then crumpled.

The second Indian used the age-old tactic of Plains warriors; with one heel hooked over the spine of his animal and clinging to the horse's mane on the off side, he fired twice in Hezekiah's direction before the terrified horse ducked his head and bucked so hard the Indian was flung away. Before either Gus or Hezekiah could locate him among the blind-running horses and dust, he disappeared beneath the hooves of many horses.

The remaining two Indians reined northward which put them not only in dust and night-gloom but on the far side of the horses.

Hezekiah yelled at Gus. "Even odds, let's go!"

By the time they had caught the horses in the corral and avoided being trampled, the last of the stolen horses had passed.

When they rigged out and left the

yard in a headlong rush about all they could make out was distant movement and sound.

They had an advantage, the stolen horses had been run hard for many miles. Here and there they passed exhausted animals standing head-hung. Others had taken advantage of not being coerced from the rear and split off running southward.

Someone up ahead fired a Winchester, the sound was sharper, more distinct than the sound of a belt gun. Hezekiah altered course in the direction of the gun-flash. Gus also altered course but not until he was several hundred yards east of the warrior.

Hezekiah did not see the bronco but Gus did and was waiting. At the last moment the Indian saw a mounted white man through dust and gloom. He hauled frantically northward. Gus shot him from a distance of about sixty yards.

Hezekiah flashed past holding his Winchester high. His horse followed the riderless animal of the man Gus had shot. Hezekiah looked neither right nor left.

Up ahead more horses veered from the main drive, so many in fact Gus had to watch closely in order to avoid a collision.

It was pandemonium, the lack of decent light made it worse. He saw Hezekiah ahead, still holding his saddle gun high.

What he didn't see because the man was kneeling on the ground, was a bloody-hand warrior tracking Hezekiah with an upraised carbine. What Gus saw was the muzzleblast. From the corner of his eye he saw Hezekiah's horse go end over end.

Gus swung off and fired his Winchester empty in the direction of the Indian. His firing was not returned. He yanked his horse in the direction where Hezekiah was lying face down. As he reached the site and knelt, someone fired at him from the place where he had shot the last warrior. He flinched and twisted. With a fired out Winchester he drew his belt gun, got flat down and waited. With a cocked six-gun inside his hat he lay sprawled with one flung-forward arm under his head.

It was a long, tense wait before he made out something dark moving against a slightly less dark background.

He would have bet his saddle he had hit that hostile but the man did not even seem to limp.

His chest had red zigzag lines painted across it. If he'd had a feather braided into his hair there was no sign of it. He was a sinewy man who moved like a cougar. As he got closer he raised his gaze from Gus to the horse. His own horse was gone.

The stolen horses were no longer in sight, even their sounds were fading.

When he was close he hesitated to consider the sprawled white man. When Gus shot him the top of Gus's hat went with the bullet. The Indian staggered backwards from impact. Gus cocked his hand gun for another shot when the Indian took two faltering steps forward and fell. Gus could have reached and touched him with one hand.

The Indian did have a feather. It was attached to a bone-hair choker around his neck. It had six notches. He had killed six men.

Gus rolled him over carefully, listened, waited a long moment then arose and led his horse where Hezekiah lay. Hezekiah's horse was nearby picking grass.

As Gus knelt Hezekiah groaned. Gus searched for the wound. There should have been blood but Gus found none until Hezekiah struggled to sit up. As Gus helped him Hezekiah turned his head slowly, saw his horse and looked at Gus. There was a thin streak of blood along the rear of Hezekiah's neck. Gus had to lean closer to find the injury and as he straightened back still supporting the large bearded man with an arm around his back Hezekiah

212

groaned again and thickly said, "What happened?"

"In'ian shot you." Gus wagged his head. If the Indian had aimed better Hezekiah would be dead. In darkness, a head shot in the predawn gloom had one chance in hundreds of hitting the head. Maybe the bronco hadn't tried a head-shot, maybe he had meant to aim lower. Under the circumstances Gus would never know about that.

He crouched with the larger man for a while before saying, "Give me your hands. When I pull, try to stand up."

It took time but Hezekiah eventually was upright. Gus braced him. Hezekiah's eyes didn't focus, he clung to Gus and mumbled something. Gus said, "Stand still. I'll get the horse."

Hezekiah was too dazed to fully understand.

It was difficult to hoist the large man into the saddle and when he was astride he leaned, groggily shook his head and mumbled again. Gus led the horse toward his own animal, got astride and began the ride back leading Hezekiah who clung to the saddle horn with both hands.

His mind did not clear until they were close to the corral, then he felt the back of his head and neck, gazed at sticky fingers and said, "Son of a bitch," very clearly.

Gus got him inside the cabin, told him to sit on his bunk and went back outside to care for the horses.

Doug slept through everything, but as sunrise approached he awakened, stared at Hezekiah and said, "What happened to you?"

"Damned In'ian shot me. The son of a bitch."

Gus returned as the sun came over the far curve of the world. He saw Doug staring, ignored him, went to the cooking area and fired up some kindling for hot coffee. He felt drained.

Later, he washed Hezekiah's wound, sprinkled some of the medicine man's powder on it and watched Hezekiah sip scalding hot coffee. Between sips

214

Hezekiah regarded Gus solemnly. "We didn't come off too good, did we?"

"We done fair," Gus replied. "Killed all four of 'em."

Hezekiah put the cup aside. "What I meant was four of us come up here with the cattle. We're down to just you."

"You'll be fine in a few days," Gus told him.

"You can't do it by yourself, Gus." Hezekiah emptied the cup before continuing. "We're whipped," he said. "Luck done turned against us. We better trail the cattle down to that town, hunt up a buyer an' quit. I feel dog-tired."

"Lie down," Gus told the big-bearded man.

They heard riders passing northward. Gus went outside. It was not a large party. The sun was above the horizon. He watched them. If they saw him they gave no indication of it. He could see roached scalplocks. Black Thunder and some Crow warriors.

He sighed, went back inside, shucked shell belt and sidearm, went to the cooking place and began to half-heartedly make a meal. Doug watched then said, "Sounded like a war. How'd you do it?"

"Got two from the corral. Run the other two down. I'll give 'em credit. They was fightin' In'ians."

"Was that the Crows passin' up yonder?"

Gus nodded. He was frying bread in bear grease. They had enough sugar to hide the taste of the grease but they were low on flour which he ordinarily would have fried the bread in.

Doug started to sit up. Hezekiah growled at him from his bunk. "Lie back you clanged fool. We don't need you bustin' them thornpins loose. *Lie back!*"

Someone scratched at the door and despite his weariness Gus reached his six-gun in five strides and wrenched the door open with the pistol rising.

Long Walker stiffened.

216

Gus let the gun sag and jerked his head. As the youth entered rays of sunlight came through the shattered window covering.

The Crow youth stared. Hezekiah growled at him. "Black Thunder after the horses, boy?"

Long Walker nodded and looked from the two men in bunks to Gus. "Black Thunder say to tell you he give you another pouch of yellow dirt."

Gus went back to his cooking. Hezekiah waited until the youth was beside his bunk then spoke. "We seen 'em passin' but wasn't no way we could get over yonder to warn Black Thunder before they got there. So we set up a bushwhack for when they come back."

There was more scratching at the door. This time when Gus opened it holding the six-gun behind his back, he stared.

Dawn Child came inside wrinkling her nose at the smell of Gus's cooking. Her eyes widened at sight of Hezekiah flat out with a bloody shirt collar. Long Walker stepped clear as his mother came to bedside looking downward.

Hezekiah said, "It ain't much. Got grazed behind the head is all."

She leaned for a closer look as she said, "Some of the cattle near our camp. Long way to travel for them."

Hezekiah was not entirely surprised. The last time he and Gus had ridden out they hadn't found some of the cattle. He gazed at the handsome woman. "Black Thunder said his folks wouldn't kill 'em for meat."

She eased him onto his side for a closer look at the injury. It was swollen but clean. She asked Long Walker for his knife, lifted Hezekiah's unshorn mane in back and with one slash cut away all that covered the wound.

Doug saw her drop the hair and said, "She lifted your scalp, Hezekiah."

He got no answer. Dawn Child wet a rag and washed Hezekiah's face with it. He offered no objection but squinted his eyes closed during the scrubbing. When she was finished she said something in Crow to Long Walker. He did not seem happy. Doug made a good guess. She was sending the youth for the old medicine man. He told her Hezekiah would be fine, they didn't need Running Dog.

She seemed to understand but spoke again to her son and this time he left the cabin.

Gus brought a tin plate to Hezekiah with three slabs of fried bread on it. Hezekiah raised a hand for the plate when Dawn Child intercepted, took the plate from Gus and put it on the table. When Gus frowned she said. "You show me. I make eating."

Doug couldn't hide his grin. Hezekiah considered the woman in silence. He had been living on fried bread for years.

Dawn Child, unfamiliar with the variety of articles and stores the Texans had, went outside where Long Walker had dumped her pad saddle and returned with a parfleche bag. The men watched in silence as she used boiling water to soak strips of withered jerky. She saw them watching, smiled and when the soup was ready she filled three tin cups, gave one to Doug, one to Gus and sat on the edge of Hezekiah's cot to hold the cup for him to drink. He took the cup from her; he had a slight headache and a sore neck but he was not an invalid.

An hour later with the sun climbing, with new-day heat coming inside, Squawman and Black Thunder arrived to the sound of horses being driven westerly some distance from the cabin's clearing.

Black Thunder's expression never changed, it was the look of leashed defiance. He ignored them all except Hezekiah.

He produced another of those little doeskin pouches and put it on Hezekiah's chest as he spoke. Squawman interpreted. "He say you good warriors. You make strong friends. He say you stay. Plenty grass, plenty water an' wood.

He say yellow dirt best he can give. You become Crows."

Hezekiah held the little pouch in one hand as he looked at the Crow spokesman. "Didn't have time to warn you. We seen 'em headin' west yestiddy."

Black Thunder did not take his eyes off the large, bearded man on the bunk as Squawman interpreted. He finally looked at the wound, listened to what Dawn Child had to say and brushed Hezekiah's arm with his hand as he told him they were brothers. "Brothers three times fought together. Brothers got back stolen horses and killed bloody hands. Brothers share this place."

By the time the tall bronco had interpreted all that, Long Walker came back inside with Running Dog who had the old army pouch slung over one shoulder. They made room for him, but he ignored Hezekiah and went to Doug's bunk where he began an examination. Occasionally he would grunt as he peeked and probed. He sprinkled more of his powder under the bandaging and spoke directly to Doug. Again the tall Indian interpreted. "He say you got no bad blood. He say you stay down an' one day when leaves fall you be good again."

Doug faintly frowned as he replied. "Old man, I'm gettin' saddle sores from lyin' in this damned bed."

Running Dog listened to Squawman then replied. Squawman put it into English — of sorts. "Running Dog say better saddle sores than bad blood." The old man made a wrinkly smile and moved to Hezekiah's bunk.

Here, his examination was brief. He spoke suddenly in English, heavily accented and with intervals between words, but understandable English. "White eyes good men. You make good Absaroke. We keep you."

Black Thunder leaned to grip Hezekiah's forearm. Hezekiah returned the clasp. They looked at one another as solemn as owls.

Black Thunder turned to Dawn
Child and told her in their own
language to stay and care for the
white-eyed Crows, after which he and
old Running Dog went out into the
rising warmth to their horses. Long
Walker followed them. From the back
of his horse Black Thunder gazed
steadily at his grandson, jutted his
chin in the direction of the log house
and rode away with Running Dog.

From the porch Squawman spoke in
Crow and Long Walker came back.
They spoke briefly before Squawman
also went out to his horse, sprang
astride and followed the pair of old
Indians. None of them looked back.

Gus doused the breakfast fire, kicked
off his boots and dropped down on his
bunk. The Second Coming could have
arrived, golden trumpets and all and he
would not have awakened.

Dawn Child found a broom made of
ripgut grass and began sweeping. She
gave curt orders to her son who helped
clean the cabin.

Doug slept but Hezekiah watched the woman and her boy. When Long Walker passed he handed him the doeskin pouch and pointed to the table.

With dusk approaching Gus went to the creek to wash, and afterward dragooned Long Walker to help him drag the dead bloodyhands out a ways and pile rocks atop them. Long Walker got two pistols, two fleshing knives and one Winchester with a pouch of bullets. The other Winchester had a shattered stock. They buried it with one of the dead hostiles.

The horses dickered. Gus took them out to grass with Long Walker as a helper, and the youth got his first lesson about driving animals to feed. Ordinarily Indians rode horses hard and fast. Not this time. Gus explained the purpose of keeping the horses in sight without frightening them.

He and Long Walker sat in boulder shadows watching the horses crop grass and talked. Long Walker did not remember his father very well, Black Thunder had been the main man in his life.

He mentioned hunts they had made together. He recalled the first time he had seen whites, he and his grandfather had sat their horses among some trees watching whites all dressed alike in blue suits riding behind two men in front with a third man carrying a little swallow-tailed flag. Black Thunder had said they were white-eyed soldiers, enemies to Indians.

He mentioned going down to that town a day's ride over land with cattle on it. He had gone with Squawman to trade yellow dirt at a store for kettles and ammunition. He remembered how the whites regarded the tall Indian and the small boy with closed faces.

Gus listened, built and lighted a smoke and thought of what Hezekiah had said, which was a fact, one man could not do it all. He gazed down where the horses were, at the miles of Mandan Mesa with its heat-hazed distance mountains and thought this was the place to settle in, hardships, short-handed and all.

If Hezekiah insisted on taking the cattle down below to sell them and after that to start wandering again, this time he and Gus would part company. For good this time.

12

A Fork in the Trail

THE Crows brought back the cattle which had probably been stampeded the day and night before. Black Thunder was not among them but Squawman was. He left his companions with the cattle, loped to the cabin to tell Hezekiah what he and his companions had done, and also told him there was a lame cow which they had left to follow at her own pace. He had no idea what ailed the cow.

Gus and Long Walker went after the cow after the Crows had left. What ailed her was a three-inch thornpin in one hoof. Long Walker helped Gus herd the old girl to the corral where Gus roped and sidelined her against the green logs. She bawled, slobbered and fought like a tiger as Gus threw his weight against her, yanked the sore foot up and pulled out the thornpin.

When they released the cow she ran as though she'd had no injury. Long Walker asked if he could hold Gus's lariat. Gus handed over the rope and after caring for their horses took Long Walker a short distance away, roped a corral post, recoiled the lass and handed it to Long Walker. Their first problem arose because while Gus was right handed, Long Walker was left handed so the lariat had to be recoiled, twisted with each loop until Long Walker could use it. They spent an hour with the lass rope. Long Walker's first attempt to master a lariat was a total failure.

Gus went through the motions slowly with dusk settling. He did this three times before handing the rope to the young Crow, whose last cast miraculously snagged an upright corral post.

When they went inside Dawn Child had the candles lighted and was working at Doug's cooking area. Doug was asleep but Hezekiah was lying perfectly still staring at the ceiling. He couldn't turn his head without pain so when Dawn Child brought his supper he thanked her without looking around.

Later, Long Walker told his mother in their own language what he had learned about the white man's rope. She smiled, looked over his head at Gus and softly nodded.

Later, with the scent and taste of autumn in the air Running Dog returned, entered the cabin without knocking, went to Hezekiah's bunk first, gestured for Hezekiah to lie face down and examined the wound. He grunted and without a word went to Doug's bunk where Hardy eyed the old man warily. Running Dog and Dawn Child exchanged words which she interpreted to Doug. "He say take out thornpins now. You heal good."

It was almost as painful when the old gnome removed the thornpins as it had been when he put them in, and there was bleeding, mostly from places where the thornpins had been.

Running Dog sprinkled his powder over the injury, dragged a bench over and sat at bedside looking at Doug as he spoke. Dawn Child put it into understandable English. "He say you can move but only inside house. You not bend, not lift things for another moon. He say white man's Big Spirit like you. No bad blood."

Doug glared. "Another damned month doin' nothin'?"

Dawn Child gravely inclined her head. During her stay with the Texans she had refused Gus's offer of his bunk. She and Long Walker slept on the floor in moth-eaten old buffalo robes.

Once, when Gus and Long Walker were out sifting through the cattle the youth said, "My mother say we stay."

Gus looked long at the boy and thought of grim old Black Thunder who had said Long Walker was his boy. He cleared his throat and did not comment.

Later, as they were heading for the clearing Long Walker mentioned the lariat and Gus gave it to him. He could use Doug's rope.

That evening while Long Walker was outside trying to rope corral posts, Gus told Hezekiah what the lad had said to him, and oddly enough, Hezekiah did not see this as a problem. He told Gus Dawn Child was lingering past the time when neither Doug or Hezekiah needed her.

Gus went outside to watch Long Walker with the lariat and was surprised how quickly the young Crow had mastered not just the rudiments of roping but had progressed until he rarely missed the corral uprights. When Gus had been his age he couldn't rope a stump from ten feet.

Dawn Child took her son on a hunt several days later and returned with an antelope, something the three Texans had difficulty fathoming because neither the woman or the boy had taken guns.

Long Walker explained. They had found a small band of antelope and Dawn Child had tied a greyish white rag to a bush. Antelope have outsized curiosities. It required most of the day for one of them to come close enough. When it did Dawn Child knocked it senseless with a rock from a sling made of forked sticks. All they'd had to do was cut the antelope's throat and start back with it.

Doug would have helped with the skinning and quartering but Dawn Child took him firmly by the arm, led him back to the cabin and scowling shook her head at him. Gus and Hezekiah waited until she had slammed the door before chuckling.

Doug turned on them. "Danged woman's takin' over!"

Hezekiah's reply made Gus give him a quick look. "Far's I'm concerned she can."

The days ran on, that faint acidy scent of drying leaves, curing grass and drying underbrush increased. Gus spent most of his time out with the cattle. He had taught Long Walker how to drift the horses to feed and how to afterwards corral them. The youth spent hours with the lariat. Once he even surprised himself by roping a running rabbit. It had to be a fluke, some of the best ropers alive could not do it, but Walker's pride was boundless.

They shortened his name to just Walker, perhaps sometime in generations long past it had meant the same thing to the whites — someone who walked a lot. It meant the same thing among Crows. His mother still called him by his Absaroke name but the Texans didn't.

Squawman, Running Dog and even Black Thunder occasionally rode over. The two older men said little but the tall Crow used his better command of the white man's language to say things that set the Texans to thinking, mainly Gus Crandal who had been worrying over the Crow woman and her son having moved in with the Texans. Squawman's opinion that since Dawn Child and her boy had not returned to the distant rancheria over a long period of time, there was talk among the Crows they might be held against their will by the Texans.

Hezekiah's reply to that was curt. "They can leave any time they're of a mind. We're mighty grateful for 'em stayin' but I expect we can make out without 'em."

It was Dawn Child who put an end to this talk. She spoke swiftly to the tall man in their language. He listened, continued to gaze at her after she had spoken and shortly thereafter rode away.

Hezekiah asked what she had said. She avoided his gaze as she replied, "I say you not all well yet. I say Absaroke men worse than squaws. Talk out of both sides of mouth."

Hezekiah and Gus exchanged a look. It was Doug who commented while puttering with the worn, dry leather of his bridle. "I need some grease for this thing," and went outside to find some where the antelope had been butchered.

The subject did not arise again, at least not among the Texans or Dawn Child.

Doug did not appear to mind that she had preempted his chores, mainly in the cooking area. He obeyed the old medicine man's admonition about exertion to the letter. Even after the wound had mended he obeyed what the medicine man had said, which amused Hezekiah and Gus, who now had a wrangler to chore with him, and who even slept with his lariat.

Doug could finally straddle a horse and followed up the creek which ran through a corner of the corral to find a fishing hole. There were few things less likely to aggravate his wound than fishing.

He located several pools, brought back fat trout wrapped in dry grass, even made himself a passable fishing pole with line made of carefully sized antelope gut.

Autumn arrived with an occasional cold wind out of the north where snow had fallen in the highlands. On a particularly warm day with sparkling visibility an Indian came to the clearing on foot. He was one of the scouts that were always patrolling. He told Dawn Child what he had seen and left in a trot. She told Hezekiah the scout had seen three white men riding in the direction of the plateau. She said the scout had told her they had a big belly with them leading the way.

Dawn Child's agitation was contagious, even somewhat stolid Hezekiah was worried. He asked Dawn Child if white men had come to the plateau before. She said only once long ago when she had been a child. They were traders with guns, blankets and iron kettles to trade for skins.

Gus rode southward to the lip of Mandan Mesa, let his horse graze and sat in dappled treeshade studying the land far below. When he saw the four riders he marvelled that the scout could make such a detailed description. All Gus could make out was that there were four of them. He could not distinguish one from another but they were clearly using the same trail the Texans had used when they had first arrived.

It would be another day before they reached the mesa. Gus rode back to report what he had seen. That evening at supper not much was said but clearly the big belly knew of the rancheria so it was reasonable to assume the three white men could be soldiers or Indian agents in which either case they would want to locate the Crow camp, and the next guess was that they would go back wherever they came from, make their report and eventually the army would come. Indians were supposed to be on reservations.

Gus recognised the hand writing on the wall. Regardless of anything the Texans could do, Black Thunder's band was in serious danger which would increase if the Indians fired on Indian agents or anyone shortly to arrive to scout up Mandan Mesa.

After supper Hezekiah jerked his head in Long Walker's direction. They went to the corral, rigged out two horses and left the cabin riding southward. Dawn Child watched her son fade into the settling dusk from the doorway. Doug told her not to worry, whatever Hezekiah was up to there was no one alive who could be relied upon more to be careful. This may not have lessened Dawn Child's anxiety, probably nothing could have; she was a mother.

Gus and Doug went to the porch to sit in gathering darkness. They were both accustomed to Hezekiah doing things without explaining why, but Gus had an idea this time about the large man's intention. He said, "If he'd rode west I'd guess he figured to warn Black Thunder. Ridin' south he's got somethin' else in mind."

Doug's response indicated that he was thinking of the worst. He said, "If he finds 'em in the dark and shoots 'em, when they don't come back to wherever they come from sure as hell there'll be others come lookin' for 'em."

Gus rolled and lighted a quirly, trickled smoke and shook his head. He would have bet his best horse Hezekiah had no intention of shooting anyone.

Dawn Child came out to join them on the bench. Her agitation was obvious even in semi-darkness. Again, Doug tried to be reassuring. She sat like stone acting as though she had not heard Doug. After a while she said Black Thunder should be warned and Gus reminded her of the scout who had first seen the horseback strangers.

Doug went out to the corral and a horse nickered at him. Somewhere in the settling night an owl hooted. All three people straightened until a second owl answered. Even then Doug returned to the porch. It was late in the season for owls to be seeking mates.

They went inside. Gus used an old army blanket to cover the window hole. Dawn Child lighted candles and Doug went to the table to begin rubbing antelope fat into his bridle.

It was after supper when Dawn Child at the cabin's door made a little trilling sound. Gus and Doug joined her. In the bright distance they saw two riders approaching. One was smaller than the other one. Dawn Child went to the porch to shade her eyes. When she spoke Gus was again impressed with the Indian capacity to clearly see what he could only indistinctly make out over a considerable distance.

When Hezekiah and the lad reached the corral and began to off-saddle, no one said a word but Dawn Child went back inside to the cooking area to fire kindling for the first meal of the day.

While still at the corral Gus and Doug watched Hezekiah put an arm around Long Walker's shoulders briefly before they both crossed to the porch.

Long Walker ducked inside where his mother waited. Hezekiah sank down on the bench, got a fresh cud tucked into his cheek and eyed the other two Texans as he slowly said, "That boy's a natural born horsethief. They had their animals hobbled in a little clearin'. He belly-crawled out there without spookin' the animals, took off the hobbles and crawled back. We was leavin' when a cougar screamed." Hezekiah's face brightened slightly. "Them horses went back down the trail like old Nick was after 'em." He stopped smiling. "They'll be back. Their kind don't give up, but not them four, at least for a long time." He arose at the smell of cooking and got as far as the door before Doug said. "Somebody better tell Black Thunder."

Hezekiah's wintry small smile returned as he said, "The Crow who screamed like a cougar will do that," and disappeared inside.

Gus wagged his head. "For a fact cougars don't hunt in the dark."

Doug agreed. "An' them four horses wouldn't know that, would they?"

Hezekiah slept, Long Walker joined Gus and Doug looking for cattle. It was another warm day but with an edge of a chill as the sun descended. Doug rooted out that bull the cougar had attacked. It was in an evil mood from flies but its injuries were healing well. He went back to find Gus and Long Walker and the three of them headed for the clearing. In the morning Doug and Long Walker took the horses out to feed. Long Walker showed Doug how handy he had become with his treasured lariat.

That night after supper they got a surprise. Hezekiah and Dawn Child went for a stroll beyond the corral. Doug said, "You don't suppose . . . "

Gus winked at Long Walker who was cleaning the weapons he had appropriated from the stronghearts. Long Walker winked back.

It was a chilly night with a harvest moon hanging up there bigger than life.

Hezekiah led off northward up the creek until he saw two huge boulders and without knowing it, when they sat they were at Doug's favourite fishing hole. He told her he did not believe those strangers would not return. She thought if they did not return soon they would be unable to reach Mandan Mesa until the following summer. "Much snow," she told him.

He studied her profile. In any position she was a handsome woman. He busied himself skiving off a fresh chew. She watched in silence. After he had cheeked the molasses-cured she asked if she could try it, and Hezekiah skived off a sliver and handed it to her.

She did as she had seen him do many times, gradually straightened on the rock and with a violent effort got rid of the tobacco. She rinsed her mouth at the creek and Hezekiah laughed. She had never heard him laugh before. She returned to the rock and said, "Worse than bad water."

He took down a deep breath, looked straight ahead and said, "How long has your man been dead?"

"Long time. Long Walker too young when he died."

Hezekiah jettisoned his cud and cleared his pipes. "You are young."

She looked at her feet. "Not very young . . . you?"

"Sixty-two years. Old. Too old."

Her gaze remained fixed on the ground. "No. Strong man. Stronger than Gus an' Doug." She abruptly raised her eyes to his face. "You want woman?"

Hezekiah, with nothing to guide him through this awkward situation, considered the creek. "Maybe I need one woman," he told

She did not lower her eyes. "All right."

Hezekiah rummaged for his pouch of molasses-cured, quit rummaging and stood up, sat down and let go a big breath.

They sat in silence for a long moment

then he looked directly at her. "You know about marryin'?"

"I know Crow way. You want to marry?"

Hezekiah again rummaged for the pouch and again rammed it back in his pocket. "Black Thunder might say no."

She smiled, "He can't say no. Not now."

"Why — not now?"

"Last time he come I ask him."

This time Hezekiah's eyes sprang wide open. She laughed. "Black Thunder need brother with hairy face. He told me now you stay, Absaroke have strong friend." She put her palm against Hezekiah's chest over the heart. "You Absaroke."

Hezekiah arose to start back; as they walked she almost timidly put her hand in his hand. Neither looked at the other until they had the cabin in sight then Hezekiah stopped and faced her. "What about Long Walker? He's Black Thunder's boy."

"No. Long Walker my boy, my son."

"Black Thunder won't like him livin' over here."

"Not at first he don't like, but he say you need a son more than he does. He say his world is dying, your world is just beginning. Long Walker go with me, your woman."

Hezekiah finally successfully cheeked a cud. When they reached the corral a horse nickered and from the darkness of the porch Gus spoke. "See any hostiles, did you?" His tone was as dry as dust. Hezekiah reddened but in darkness, with his beard, it was not noticeable.

He and Dawn Child remained at the corral after Doug and Gus had gone inside. The only other user of the bench would have joined the people at the corral but Doug reached through the door, snagged Long Walker by the shoulder and jerked him inside after which Doug closed the door.

The following day Black Thunder

arrived with Running Dog and Squawman. Each Indian was attired in his ceremonial smoked-tans.

When they entered the cabin they were as solemn as owls. Squawman spoke quietly. "Our scout saw you, watched Long Walker turn loose the horses. He screamed like a cougar. Black Thunder say you best friend of Absaroke. He come to share blood with you. Make you Crow."

Hezekiah looked quickly in Dawn Child's direction. She walked over to him, pulled up his right sleeve and stepped aside. Black Thunder and Running Dog came close, the spokesman nodded and old Running Dog raised Black Thunder's sleeve to the elbow and drew his fleshing knife.

Dawn Child laid a hand lightly on Hezekiah as the wizened old man made two shallow cuts, used a strip of doeskin to bind the arms and stepped back, said something to Black Thunder whose eyes with their muddy whites never left Hezekiah's face.

Squawman placed his palm against Hezekiah's chest. "Brothers."

When the old man removed the doeskin neither scratch bled. Hezekiah lowered his sleeve, throughout the entire ritual he was thinking of something he felt had to be said to the Crow spokesman. First, he said it to Squawman who interpreted it to Black Thunder whose fixed gaze on Hezekiah's face never wavered.

Black Thunder replied to Squawman in few words. Squawman did not interpret, he nodded at Dawn Child who interpreted. "Black Thunder say it is done."

"What's done?" Hezekiah asked.

"I am your woman."

Hezekiah faced Black Thunder. "Squawman tell him I'm much obliged. I will be good to her an' the boy."

As Squawman was interpreting the spokesman fished inside his silvery grey shirt, drew forth another of those small doeskin pouches and dropped it into

Hezekiah's hand as he spoke.

This time Dawn Child did not await Squawman's interpretation. She said, "My father say white man with big belly return. Not after snow gets deep. The people have many moon to make up mind to move or be led away like tame cows to a reservation. He say he want you to sit in the councils."

Hezekiah soberly inclined his head. "Let me know when an' I'll ride over."

After the Indians departed Hezekiah took Dawn Child as far as the corral to tell her what he thought. "Now they know about the rancheria the whites will come back. Most likely next time with many soldiers."

She said, "Black Thunder know that."

He looked down into her face. "If he fights it'll be a massacre. Soldiers use big guns — cannon."

She nodded. "He know that too."

"Then they got no choice."

"One," she replied. "Go north to Canada."

Hezekiah leaned on the topmost stringer. "Then he better not wait 'til spring."

"You say that at council. It is cold."

They returned to the cabin where Doug sat stonily silent with his greased bridle. He and Gus looked up when Hezekiah came inside. Doug, usually the first to speak, said, "Hezekiah, I got no taste for fightin' against our own people."

Hezekiah repeated what he had told Dawn Child at the corral, Doug fiddled with the bridle a moment then said, "I expect we owe the In'ians." He stood up looking at Gus. "I never been that far north. Gus, you know where Canada is?"

Gus shook his head as he said, "We could talk to folks on the way. There's bound to be towns up north." He considered Hezekiah, Long Walker and Dawn Child. "I'll come back. Like Doug said, we owe the Crows that much. Hezekiah, can you handle things until next summer?"

Long Walker spoke for the first time. "We can."

The following morning Hezekiah and Dawn Child rode to the rancheria, councilled with Black Thunder and the Crow elders and returned to the cabin, arriving there after dark to find that during their absence Doug and Gus had rolled their blankets, filled their saddle-bags and when Hezekiah told them Black Thunder accepted them on the long ride, the three of them emptied the jug that night. The following dawn Hezekiah, Dawn Child and Long Walker watched Gus and Doug leave the yard riding west.

THE END

FIGHTING RAMROD
Charles N. Heckelmann

Most men would have cut their losses, but Frazer counted the bullets in his guns and said he'd soak the range in blood before he'd give up another inch of what was his.

LONE GUN
Eric Allen

Smoke Blackbird had been away too long. The Lequires had seized the Blackbird farm, forcing the Indians and settlers off, and no one seemed willing to fight! He had to fight alone.

THE THIRD RIDER
Barry Cord

Mel Rawlins wasn't going to let anything stand in his way. His father was murdered, his two brothers gone. Now Mel rode for vengeance.

ARIZONA DRIFTERS
W. C. Tuttle

When drifting Dutton and Lonnie Steelman decide to become partners they find that they have a common enemy in the formidable Thurston brothers.

TOMBSTONE
Matt Braun

Wells Fargo paid Luke Starbuck to outgun the silver-thieving stagecoach gang at Tombstone. Before long Luke can see the only thing bearing fruit in this eldorado will be the gallows tree.

HIGH BORDER RIDERS
Lee Floren

Buckshot McKee and Tortilla Joe cut the trail of a border tough who was running Mexican beef into Texas. They stopped the smuggler in his tracks.

BRETT RANDALL, GAMBLER
E. B. Mann

Larry Day had the choice of running away from the law or of assuming a dead man's place. No matter what he decided he was bound to end up dead.

THE GUNSHARP
William R. Cox

The Eggerleys weren't very smart. They trained their sights on Will Carney and Arizona's biggest blood bath began.

THE DEPUTY OF SAN RIANO
Lawrence A. Keating and
Al. P. Nelson

When a man fell dead from his horse, Ed Grant was spotted riding away from the scene. The deputy sheriff rode out after him and came up against everything from gunfire to dynamite.

FARGO: MASSACRE RIVER
John Benteen

The ambushers up ahead had now blocked the road. Fargo's convoy was a jumble, a perfect target for the insurgents' weapons!

SUNDANCE: DEATH IN THE LAVA
John Benteen

The Modoc's captured the wagon train and its cargo of gold. But now the halfbreed they called Sundance was going after it . . .

HARSH RECKONING
Phil Ketchum

Five years of keeping himself alive in a brutal prison had made Brand tough and careless about who he gunned down . . .

FARGO: PANAMA GOLD
John Benteen

With foreign money behind him, Buckner was going to destroy the Panama Canal before it could be completed. Fargo's job was to stop Buckner.

FARGO:
THE SHARPSHOOTERS
John Benteen

The Canfield clan, thirty strong were raising hell in Texas. Fargo was tough enough to hold his own against the whole clan.

PISTOL LAW
Paul Evan Lehman

Lance Jones came back to Mustang for just one thing — revenge! Revenge on the people who had him thrown in jail.

HELL RIDERS
Steve Mensing

Wade Walker's kid brother, Duane, was locked up in the Silver City jail facing a rope at dawn. Wade was a ruthless outlaw, but he was smart, and he had vowed to have his brother out of jail before morning!

DESERT OF THE DAMNED
Nelson Nye

The law was after him for the murder of a marshal — a murder he didn't commit. Breen was after him for revenge — and Breen wouldn't stop at anything . . . blackmail, a frameup . . . or murder.

DAY OF THE COMANCHEROS
Steven C. Lawrence

Their very name struck terror into men's hearts — the Comancheros, a savage army of cutthroats who swept across Texas, leaving behind a bloodstained trail of robbery and murder.

SUNDANCE: SILENT ENEMY
John Benteen

A lone crazed Cheyenne was on a personal war path. They needed to pit one man against one crazed Indian. That man was Sundance.

LASSITER
Jack Slade

Lassiter wasn't the kind of man to listen to reason. Cross him once and he'll hold a grudge for years to come — if he let you live that long.

LAST STAGE TO GOMORRAH
Barry Cord

Jeff Carter, tough ex-riverboat gambler, now had himself a horse ranch that kept him free from gunfights and card games. Until Sturvesant of Wells Fargo showed up.

McALLISTER
ON THE
COMANCHE CROSSING
Matt Chisholm

The Comanche, McAllister owes them a life — and the trail is soaked with the blood of the men who had tried to outrun them before.

QUICK-TRIGGER COUNTRY
Clem Colt

Turkey Red hooked up with Curly Bill Graham's outlaw crew. But wholesale murder was out of Turk's line, so when range war flared he bucked the whole border gang alone . . .

CAMPAIGNING
Jim Miller

Ambushed on the Santa Fe trail, Sean Callahan is saved by two Indian strangers. But there'll be more lead and arrows flying before the band join Kit Carson against the Comanches.

GUNSLINGER'S RANGE
Jackson Cole

Three escaped convicts are out for revenge. They won't rest until they put a bullet through the head of the dirty snake who locked them behind bars.

RUSTLER'S TRAIL
Lee Floren

Jim Carlin knew he would have to stand up and fight because he had staked his claim right in the middle of Big Ike Outland's best grass.

THE TRUTH ABOUT SNAKE RIDGE
Marshall Grover

The troubleshooters came to San Cristobal to help the needy. For Larry and Stretch the turmoil began with a brawl and then an ambush.

WOLF DOG RANGE
Lee Floren

Will Ardery would stop at nothing, unless something stopped him first — like a bullet from Pete Manly's gun.

DEVIL'S DINERO
Marshall Grover

Plagued by remorse, a rich old reprobate hired the Texas Troubleshooters to deliver a fortune in greenbacks to each of his victims.

GUNS OF FURY
Ernest Haycox

Dane Starr, alias Dan Smith, wanted to close the door on his past and hang up his guns, but people wouldn't let him.

DONOVAN
Elmer Kelton

Donovan was supposed to be dead. Uncle Joe Vickers had fired off both barrels of a shotgun into the vicious outlaw's face as he was escaping from jail. Now Uncle Joe had been shot — in just the same way.

CODE OF THE GUN
Gordon D. Shirreffs

MacLean came riding home, with saddle tramp written all over him, but sewn in his shirt-lining was an Arizona Ranger's star.

GAMBLER'S GUN LUCK
Brett Austen

Gamblers seldom live long. Parker was a hell of a gambler. It was his life — or his death . . .

ORPHAN'S PREFERRED
Jim Miller

Sean Callahan answers the call of the Pony Express and fights Indians and outlaws to get the mail through.

DAY OF THE BUZZARD
T. V. Olsen

All Val Penmark cared about was getting the men who killed his wife.

THE MANHUNTER
Gordon D. Shirreffs

Lee Kershaw knew that every Rurale in the territory was on the lookout for him. But the offer of $5,000 in gold to find five small pieces of leather was too good to turn down.

RIFLES ON THE RANGE
Lee Floren

Doc Mike and the farmer stood there alone between Smith and Watson. There was this moment of stillness, and then the roar would start. And somebody would die . . .

HARTIGAN
Marshall Grover

Hartigan had come to Cornerstone to die. He chose the time and the place, and Main Street became a battlefield.

SUNDANCE: OVERKILL
John Benteen

When a wealthy banker's daughter was kidnapped by the Cheyenne, he offered Sundance $10,000 to rescue the girl.

RIDE A LONE TRAIL
Gordon D. Shirreffs

The valley was about to explode into open range war. All it needed was the fuse and Ken Macklin was it.

HARD MAN WITH A GUN
Charles N. Heckelmann

After Bob Keegan lost the girl he loved and the ranch he had sweated blood to build, he had nothing left but his guts and his guns but he figured that was enough.

SUNDANCE: IRON MEN
Peter McCurtin

Sundance, assigned to save the railroad from a murder spree, soon came to realise that he'd have to fight fire with fire, bullets with bullets and death with death!